elephants in the room

PRAISE FOR ELEPHANTS IN THE ROOM

"Betty Jane Hegerat tells her stories with intense care and in a soft-voiced, clear way that is lean on descriptions, explanations, and emotional fireworks . . . In this collection, Hegerat examines with admirable restraint the serious and mostly unanswerable questions about living the ordinary life with dignity and kindness. This is a book to be loved."

SHARON BUTALA, AWARD-WINNING AUTHOR OF
LEAVING WISDOM

"Betty Jane Hegerat is a meticulous observer of the human condition, and the family in particular. The stories in Elephants in the Room *are written with succinct, unadorned prose and a gentleness that belies the strength of their messages. With warmth, humour, empathy, and intimacy, her characters search for the connection and remembrance we seek in those moments of heartbreak that punctuate all of our lives. A most moving collection of short fiction."*

LORI HAHNEL, AUTHOR OF *FLICKER AND VERMIN:*
STORIES

*"*Elephants in the Room *is a gorgeously beguiling collection. Individual stories are beautifully paced, with a skilful interplay between past and present. Delightful."*

PETER MIDGELY, WRITER, EDITOR, AND TRANSLATOR

elephants
in the
room

New short fiction by
Betty Jane Hegerat

SHADOWPAW
PRESS

ELEPHANTS IN THE ROOM
By Betty Jane Hegerat

Trade Paperback ISBN: 978-1-998273-48-5
Ebook ISBN: 978-1-998273-49-2

Shadowpaw Press
Regina, Saskatchewan, Canada
www.shadowpawpress.com

Made possible through Creative Saskatchewan's
Book Publishing Production Publishers' Stream Program

CONTENTS

THE QUEEN IS COMING

MY MOTHER PHONES at eight o'clock in the morning on March 27. "Charlie! The Queen is coming for the big celebration. I want to go to the party," she says.

It takes me a minute to register that she's referring to Alberta's one hundredth anniversary as a province. "Too crowded, Mom," I mumble.

"You sound sleepy, son."

I've given up reminding her that I work nights. I do data entry at a bank. Suits me well, and I'm free to ferry Ma to medical appointments and funerals—pretty much her only outings these days.

I'd cruelly hoped, when I heard about the pending royal visit on CBC Radio this morning, that Ma would be having one of her bad days. That the news wouldn't penetrate the fog.

"You know I hate crowds," I tell her.

"You're fifty-seven years old," she says. "You should get over these little fears of yours." She sighs. "This will be my last chance to see her."

My mother's obsession with the Royal Family began in 1948 when she and Princess Elizabeth were both pregnant. I was born two days after the little prince. If the royal had been a girl, I would have been named Ernest, for my father.

"The tickets are free," she says. "All you have to do is get in line." I imagine her head trembling as she speaks. "I hope I can find my hat."

In Ma's royal album, there is a picture from 1951. The two of us standing on Ninth Avenue, Ma in a dark wool coat, matching felt hat with a brim and feather. Me, buttoned into a heavy brown coat cut down from Ernest's overcoat just a few months after he had died in a streetcar accident. I'm clutching a small Union Jack in my chubby fist.

The princess was wearing a mink coat that day, and a matching hat that hugged her head. Ma had a milliner fashion a replica of that mink cloche hat out of a piece of fur no one has ever identified. My sister, Annie, swears it's cat. The hat has only ever been worn for royal viewings. Four in all.

I grudgingly agree to get tickets to the Saddledome reception. But I oversleep on the morning they go up.

Ma is surprisingly cheerful. "Never mind. I'm not sure I could have endured the program. They say it will be hours long."

"Right!" I say in jovial response. I've had nightmares about chasing her runaway wheelchair down ramps. About the accidents to which this proud woman is now prone and the mortification of both of us.

"We'll just go down to the public viewing," Ma says. "Maybe she'll do a walkabout." She's getting excited now. "Wouldn't it be wonderful if Charles were coming?"

"Don't know why he isn't," I say. "He's fifty-seven. He probably loves riding around with his mother."

"He's busy," she snaps. "He's getting married again, you know."

Ma loved Diana, is sour on Camilla, but says at least Charlie Windsor isn't going to remain an old bachelor for the rest of his life. And he has those two fine sons. I, on the other hand, allowed a childless marriage to wash up on the rocks ten years ago.

The weather in the week leading up to the Queen's arrival in Calgary is cold, grey, and fiercely windy. Not the sort of climate to which a responsible man would expose his frail eighty-two-year-old mother.

But she insists. My sister, Annie, insists. "For gawd's sake, Chuck!" she snarls over the phone, "I offered to take her myself, but she wants you."

I slump in my chair, thinking about the hat I retrieved from the top of the closet. Even after my heroic attempts to fluff it up, the old relic looked like roadkill. I winced when Ma settled it over her scant curls and peered into the mirror. "Oh, Charlie," she whispered, "I look so old." But I, standing behind her chair, was staring at my own reflection. A fat, balding man who would never be mistaken for a prince.

Even though it's a morning in May, Ma is bundled into her black winter coat, feet encased in fur-lined boots, hat perched on her freshly permed hair. A policeman stands in the middle of Ninth Avenue, diverting traffic. Despite his shouts, I creep forward, waving my "handicapped parking" sticker. He shakes his head, but points to a loading zone around the corner.

I push Ma's wheelchair to a curbside spot in front of the Palliser Hotel. Huddled into my windbreaker, I wish I'd worn my own winter jacket. But then, just minutes before the entourage is due, the sun breaks through. Ma twists in the chair to look up at me, her face tiny beneath the fur. "They say she never wears a hat twice."

Suddenly, there's a limo approaching, and as it glides by, a smattering of applause from the crowd. A blur of face, a wave. Finished in seconds. Ma doesn't blink. "That's not her," she says. "It's that Clarkson woman."

The governor general, Ma tells me, is going ahead to stage the receiving line for the Queen and Prince Philip. It's the way things work.

I'm eyeing the corner of Ninth and Macleod, a block away, thinking that this is where the cars will slow. Which is why the crowd is thickest there. For the better view. I hope my mother doesn't notice that I haven't chosen the best vantage point. Haven't even tried.

She turns again and motions for me to listen. I crouch beside the chair. "You look at her face, Charlie. She's so... serene. How can that be possible with all the stress the poor woman has been through?"

I choke back a snort. "She has a bit of hired help, Ma."

"Oh, not that," she says. "It's the children. The way they live their lives. What a disappointment that must be."

I feel heavy, leaning there on my haunches, the weight of my own dull life hovering over Ma and me. "I guess that's just something that comes with being a mother," I say.

"No, dear," she tells me softly, without taking her eyes off the street. "Elizabeth has had bad luck with her Charles. Aren't I a lucky old woman to have raised a decent man like you?" She turns now, and the smile takes twenty years from her face.

I can see cars approaching, people waving and cheering in the next block. Too fast. They'll be past us in a flash. I crank Ma's chair around, bounce it off the curb and race down the street, Ma gasping and waving her arms.

"Make way!" I shout. "The Queen is coming!" At the corner, the crowd parts to let us pop up onto the sidewalk just before the second limo in the procession slows and glides past. Under a big-brimmed white hat, a smiling face turns to Ma, a gloved hand makes an elegant salute.

Ma grabs my arm. "She smiled right into my face!"

I bend, press my cheek to hers. "Of course," I say. "She recognized the hat."

UNMASKED

THERE WERE no vacant benches in the park, so I leaned against a tree. I watched the masked parents riding herd on their unmasked little bandits—no way were those kids safe-distancing on the playground equipment. I was glad Bridget hadn't suggested a coffee shop where I'd have to take off my mask between sips of coffee. Bridget was not in my bubble.

Never in the past twenty years had I expected this rendezvous would happen. I was listed as "father unknown" on the birth registration and adoption information. Inge phoned after the baby was born to tell me this, just in case my family had any intention of interfering with her plans. As if. My dad said I should be relieved. If I had been named and Inge had decided to keep the baby, I could end up paying support for years. In spite of feeling relieved—no longer having my nuts caught in a noose, as Dad so delicately put it—my teenage mind took a secret swaggering pride in knowing I'd fathered a kid.

"How do you even know the kid is yours?" Dad said. Mom claimed I'd been lured. Dad liked "entrapment." "For Chrissake, you're only seventeen years old."

I glanced over at a guy kicking around a soccer ball with a small boy who fell down every time he swung his foot too wide.

The dad? He looked about my age. No parents in this group looked like they should have been in a high school physics class. When I was seventeen, little kids made me nervous.

I tugged at the brim of my tweed cap; this was the rose on my lapel that I'd told Bridget to look for. No sign yet of the yellow jacket she said she'd be wearing.

What was I feeling? Curious, and shaken. I was curious about how she'd tracked me down. Inge was the only possibility. She'd found Inge, and Inge declared me "known," complete with contact info? But why? Shaken because this was a strong female voice, not the whisper of a baby ghost.

Other than my mom and dad, the only person who knew this little bit of my past was my husband. I'd told Tyrone because I didn't want any secrets between us. He'd actually shuddered. "I hope you don't mean that because you're proven breeding stock, you want to find a mama vessel to produce one for us?" No! When we decided to get married, neither of us pictured a future as daddies.

"My name is Bridget," she'd said when she phoned. "You're my birth father. Can we meet?"

I was surprised that I didn't hesitate. Tyrone told me I should have squeaked out. "Wrong number," and hung up.

Tyrone was not the least bit curious about my phantom daughter. "So, your secret's out—now put it to rest. Go meet her, tell her you had an experimental fling and left some sperm behind, and find out what she wants. Maybe she's planning on having a kid herself and is checking to make sure there aren't any genetic horrors in your family medical history."

Ah, yes, the sperm that got away. In Grade 10 CALM class—Career and Life Management—the boys were filtered out for Sex Ed, and we got to watch Mr. Spencer's demonstration of "safe sex." With bad running commentary, he stretched a condom over a peeled banana. I found out with Inge that it wasn't as easy as it looked. My fruit wasn't nearly as compliant as a banana.

Inge worked in my mom's bookstore. She was taking time off

to make enough money for her next year of university. Mom thought this was a great arrangement for the summer; if I worked in the store as well, she didn't need to be there every day. Surely Inge and I could look after the shop.

We got along famously. In the beginning, just playing around, flirty comments. But then, "Just a bit of fun," Inge said.

How could I decline a free-spirited blonde *woman*? Inge was twenty. I was a virgin, curious about women, and too shy to dare flirt with a couple of guys who'd been sending signals.

When I look back now and remember Inge's teasing and laughter, I blush at the thought of her treating me like a pet. We did the deed maybe a half dozen times in all. During the last time, Mom made an unexpected appearance just to be sure that all was well. When she quietly opened the door to the back room, things were going very well.

Maybe if I'd been twenty and Inge seventeen, Mom would at least have given her a reference.

I'd gone out to get lunch when Inge stopped by the store on a Saturday three months later. When I got back, Mom was standing behind the counter with her arms folded and a stricken look on her face. "It appears," she said, "that I'm going to be a grandma." She turned away then and fumbled in a drawer for a tissue, blew her nose, and went into the back room, leaving me and Inge alone.

"And you are going to be a daddy," Inge said, glaring at me, and I was young and stupid enough to feel like I was to blame. Even guilty. "But don't even imagine that I want you anywhere in this picture."

I never did imagine myself in that picture, but I admit that I wondered whether the baby would look like me. In the years that followed, if I thought of it at all, I'd always imagined a boy.

The wind had picked up, and a lot of parents were rallying their kids to leave. There was a bench free, and I moved onto it. Not two minutes later, someone in a blue hoodie who'd been hanging around the fringes came toward me.

"Eldon?"

I stood up and, from our safe social distance, I saw brown eyes sandwiched between a black mask and the hood of her sweatshirt. "I've been watching for a yellow jacket."

She shrugged. "I wanted to get a look at you before you saw me."

I sat down on the end of the bench. She sat in the middle. Too close. I wriggled down so far that my ass was hanging over the edge. She shook her head and slid to the other end. "We're outside, wearing masks, and I have no intention of touching you."

"Oh, no. No. I'm not afraid of that." It wasn't the virus I feared. Ever since the phone call, I'd been afraid of what she might want from me. What she would think of me.

"Bridget," I said. Where to go after that pronouncement?

She nodded slowly.

"That's a pretty name." Bridget sounded like a name Inge would have chosen. I had no idea if people changed a baby's name when they adopted it.

Silence. Brown eyes staring at me. What was I supposed to do next? Ask questions? About what? Bridget and her life were one big question mark.

"So. I guess you want some information—medical history and like that?"

"Yeah, something like that." She shrugged.

Ouch. I hadn't been expecting a joyful reunion. I didn't know what to expect, but her voice and the way she was looking at me —indifference. So why was she here?

"I'm curious about how you found me. Was it through Inge?"

She tilted her head and blinked at me.

Of course it was Inge, dumbass. Who else could point her in this direction?

Finally, she nodded.

"Where is Inge living?"

"Vancouver."

"She was keen to be a teacher back . . . in those days. I hope that worked out for her." I had to get my mouth off autopilot. This was *not* about Inge. Bridget called because she wanted to meet me. Obviously, she had questions. So let *her* ask the questions.

"She *is* a teacher."

"What . . ." No, that full stop either meant that she had no intention of sharing Inge's business with me, or that she had limited information. Memory told me Inge would have been a success no matter what she did. Whereas I was right here, exactly where I'd been twenty years ago. I clamped my jaw behind the mask. From the pull of the muscles in my cheeks, I knew I was squinting. How the hell do you make eyes smile when the rest of the face is hidden? I hadn't a clue what Bridget's eyes were saying.

"And what about you, Bridget? Are you still in school?"

"I'm taking a couple of gap years. Not sure where I'm going next."

What did she know about me? Inge could have told her that I was a little shit and my family was the bigger pile, but that didn't sound like Inge. I was sweating under the rim of the damn cap. I took it off and ran my fingers through my hair before I clamped it back on.

"What do you do for a living?" Bridget finally asked. "I know you used to work in a bookstore." So she did have more of the story than just my name.

"Actually, I still do. My mom owns the store, but I manage the place." If she were looking for any kind of financial help, she'd know a small indie bookstore wasn't the place to go.

Should I tell her Grandma had MS and couldn't get around well enough to work? Maybe she needed to know because of the medical history stuff. Maybe I'd just offer to write it all down for her. Maybe she had some kind of sheet for me to fill in. *Maybe I should get us the hell out of this interview. Ask her directly what she wants — what Tyrone said.*

"Where do *you* live, Bridget?"

"In Vancouver."

"Did you grow up in Vancouver?"

"Yessss . . ." As in "Duh."

The blue hood slipped backwards. She wasn't blonde, and there were no bouncy Inge-type curls escaping.

"Wow. Have you and Inge been in the same city all this time? That must have been a surprise."

She cocked her head to the side, and I had the feeling that under the mask, she was looking at me like I just fell off the turnip truck.

"Look, I'm sorry if I keep sticking my paw in my mouth, but I'm kind of lost here."

"You're surprised that I've lived with my mother all my life?"

"No, no. I just . . ."

What the fuck? Inge kept the baby? Did Bridget know that Inge considered giving her up? My mom wondered, a few months after the baby was born, who might have adopted her, and where they might live. My dad said she needed to do herself a favour and stop wondering. I'd wondered too, but only briefly. Until the phone call and what might come out at this meeting.

I squirmed on the bench and pulled my cap lower, trying to hide while I found a way to wriggle out of this gaffe. I felt a flash of anger at Inge. Had she deliberately misled me by mentioning adoption forms? Planned all along to keep the baby, but wanted to keep me imagining an abandoned child?

"Well, I never knew exactly what Inge's plans were. Oh, hell, Bridget. I barely knew your mom, and I never imagined I'd meet you. What can I say?"

I had a lump in my throat. I could have said I was so glad that she called . . . go full drama queen. But I *was* glad.

She pulled a wad of folded papers out of the pouch of her sweatshirt. "Actually, I have questions for you." She held up a pen.

She wanted me to fill it out here? *Don't sign anything!* I still heard my dad's raspy voice. *You know something, Dad? You might actually like this girl. She's right up front—no bullshit. Just like you.*

"The medical history you mentioned in about the second sentence after you saw me." The papers shook in her hand. It hadn't occurred to me that she might be more nervous about this meeting than I was. I had the urge to put my hand on her arm, to steady it. To touch her?

"Right. Sure. Whatever you want to know." I looked across the street at a Starbucks, where people were huddled at the outdoor tables. Oddly, I wasn't ready to walk away. Maybe we *could* sit down at one of those tables and have coffee while I answer the question.

She shook her head. "I have to go soon. Listen, I'll send these to you. You can send them back.

"Oh, one more thing," she said, and stood up. "Could you stand over there?" She pointed to the trash basket at the end of the bench. That put us at least ten feet apart. "Could you take off the mask? And the hat?"

A picture. She wanted a picture of me. I slapped the cap against my side and let it dangle from my hand. I ran my fingers through my hair again. I wished I had a comb. I wished I had better hair.

She pulled out her phone and stared at the screen. A couple of clicks, and it was back in her pocket.

"Fair's fair," I said. "How about you take off your mask?"

A shrug, a flip of the hood, and then she unhooked the mask from her ears.

I stared at her, wishing I was still wearing *my* mask so she couldn't see my chin drop and the big O of my mouth.

Holy shit. She looked like my mother. Like my sister would have looked if I had a sister.

I'd never doubted, in spite of all my dad's ranting, that there were other possible fathers. But seeing Bridget's face sent a jolt of certainty through me that this girl, this young woman, was a whole lot more than I'd imagined encountering.

Bridget began to mask herself again. "Wait! I'd like to have your picture?"

She tossed her head to flip the bangs off her forehead and tucked a strand of hair behind her ear. Big, wide-open eyes and a slight curve of a smile. "Beautiful," I said.

Suddenly, so many questions I wanted to ask her.

"Bridget, before you walk away, can we talk a bit more? I want to know more about you."

She took out her phone and glanced at it.

Checking the time? Another appointment?

She sat again but poised to go. "What do you want to know?"

"I was thinking more of another visit, maybe a more comfortable place."

She shook her head. "I'm not here for long."

Even though the sun was slipping through the clouds, the air felt much colder now. "Then I guess you have pretty much all you need."

"Pretty much. And that medical history? I'll attach it to a text, and you can get it back to me that way. I didn't put a return address on it, because I'm not sure where I'll be."

Why not c/o Inge? "Sure, if that works better." I took a deep breath. "So, you know a little about me. I don't plan on working in a dying bookstore forever. I have an English degree and plan to get some more education. I'm married. We don't have kids." Her mask was still off, and so was mine. She was looking at me intently. "I'm queer."

"I knew that," she said. Inge knew, and she'd been playing with me even more than I thought? "But thanks for telling me anyway." Bridget put her hands in her pockets and turned to go. But then stopped and looked back. "I'll think about it, Eldon. Maybe I'll phone you again sometime."

On my way out of the park, I paused to lean against the same tree. I could still see her, a small figure in the distance. I was sure, though, that I saw her turn and wave. I was sure of that.

DRESSED FOR THE OCCASION

I WAS TRYING to decide what to wear for the wedding when Catherine called. "Don't sweat it, Mom. Keeping it simple, remember? You were with us when we bought our dresses." I was indeed, and had to agree that the black trousers and beaded black tunic that Jo, my daughter-in-law-to-be, had found at the Thrift Store for forty-five dollars were simple and attractive, too.

As Catherine chattered on about the wedding venue and the menu, I dug through the top drawer of my dresser and landed on a string of pearls in a blue box. I was only half listening to Catherine. She and Jo had been vacillating between a picnic site near the river and our backyard with easy access to the basement in case of rain. They'd settled on platters of something or other from a good friend who was a vegan caterer. Catherine was going to stop by on her way home from work one day soon and bring samples.

"Mom? Are you still there?"

I took the pearls out of the bag and let them run through my fingers. "Yes. Just got distracted looking for something to brighten up this grey dress. Or maybe I just need a brighter dress."

"Nah, that's a classy number. What kind of brightness do you want?"

"At the moment, I'm holding pearls."

"I didn't know you had pearls."

"They're your grandmother's."

"Are they real pearls?"

"They're in a Birks box, so I'm assuming they are."

"Are you going to wear them?"

"No, I wouldn't feel right wearing them." Margaret would not be at the wedding, but she had a very personal attachment to this necklace. "On the other hand... "

Catherine was a step ahead of me. "You're not going to suggest that I wear them? Not my thing, Mom. Pearls make me think of oysters, and oysters make me sick."

I coiled the pearls back into the box. Catherine's grandmother, in a lucid moment, would have insisted Catherine wear the pearls and done up the clasp herself, brooking no nonsense about oysters.

Now I'm pondering a locket that was my *own* mother's. Catherine loved it when she was a little girl, and I'd promised that it would be hers one day. The day was coming soon. The pearls could go to someone else in the family. Cousins? Not likely. Certainly not for sentimental reasons. Margaret was a difficult woman, not a favourite aunt by any stretch. I had begun to refer to Margaret, although not directly, by her given name.

WHEN PAUL AND I MARRIED, I asked his mother what she would like me to call her now that we were both Mrs. with the same surname. Without hesitation, she answered, "Mom." She said that she did *not* like this new fashion of children using their parents' first names. I stuck to "you," or a clearing of the throat, an "ahem," when I wanted her attention and she wasn't looking my way. "Mom" belonged to *my* mother.

Paul's father had died when he was too young to have any memory of the man, but family gossip had told me that, short as it was, the marriage had been a joyless one. As a widow, his mother lived through years of hard scrabble, no extravagance nor luxury. She was a woman who could part with nothing, and whose hoarding we met full on when it was time to close down her house and help her move to the nursing home. By then, she was so far gone in the foggy world of dementia that Paul and I made the decisions about her belongings.

We filled dozens of green bags with clothing none of us had ever seen her wear, many items still tagged with Thrift Store prices. We dumped dusty jars of home-canned peaches and grey pickled beans that had been on the basement shelf at least twenty years beyond their best-before date.

There were albums of old family photos, and though there were glimpses of the odd brooch or piece of costume jewellery, for every special occasion, it was the pearls that adorned Margaret's "best" dress of the time.

I'd held up a child's jewellery box with a dancing ballerina—a gift our Catherine chose for Grandma—and told Paul, "She should have this. The box will brighten the top of that chest of drawers."

"Look," I said, when I spread the little sparkly collection on the bed in her new home. "Do you remember who gave this box to you?"

She'd picked up the pieces one by one, squinting at them, and tossed them back onto the bed. "Whose are these?"

"Mom," Paul said, looking her in the eye, looking for a glint of recognition, "all of this is yours." He draped the pearls over his hand. "You love this necklace."

"Take it away. It's not mine. I don't want someone else's junk."

"Why don't I keep the pearls for now? You can decide some other time where you would like them to go," I said.

She clamped her lips tight and closed her eyes. While I

scooped everything into a plastic bag, she leaned back on the pillows. "Do whatever you want."

We wound up the ballerina and left while she pirouetted to the music.

Two weeks later, someone from the nursing home called to say that Margaret was terribly upset and insisting that someone had come into her room and stolen her "jewels." She kept picking up the pink box and winding and winding the dancer until finally the mechanism jammed. We took it away on our next visit.

BY CATHERINE'S NEXT CALL, all was settled. They'd take their chances on the weather and tie the knot on the riverbank. Wasn't rain on a wedding day supposed to bring good luck? Something about wet knots being hard to untie.

"How is Grandma?" she asked.

"The same, maybe a little worse since the last time you saw her."

"Aw, that's so sad. Do you think Jo and I should visit and tell her about the wedding? Or will Dad do that? Or will you?"

I answered, "No," without hesitation. If Margaret were still of whole mind and was told that her granddaughter was marrying a woman, she'd be on the phone to her priest, asking for an intervention. In her current state of mind, this news would confuse and upset her if it penetrated the fog. There was nothing to be gained, no coherent blessing to be given.

TWO WEEKS LATER, Grandma Margaret died. She was alone in her dying, much as she had been, or perceived herself to be, all her life, in spite of her frequent visits. For ten years, we'd lived two hours away, and she would take the bus and often stay with us for a week or more. There was initial joy over seeing Paul and especially Catherine. But it was soon overlain with so much complaint that I couldn't wait to put her back on the bus for home.

Margaret was always huddled into herself for warmth. Even in mid-summer, she kept the windows shut tight, the rest of us rolling our eyes and fanning ourselves with magazines. At our house, she begged for an extra sweater, a pair of warm socks. On an occasion when she was barely four years old, Catherine stripped off her clothes and ran through the house, arms flying. A windmill, she said, to cool us down. Margaret was offended by the child's nakedness.

And she was offended by the way I did the laundry. I didn't iron. She would pull her son's shirts out of the neatly folded laundry pile and take them to him, pressed and on hangers, for his thanks. I didn't cook potatoes frequently enough for the "Irish" in her, and presumably in her son and grandchild as well. She would be at the sink peeling while the lasagna baked.

I'd expected to feel relief at her passing. For Margaret, because she was finally free of the nightmares, paranoia, and medication that had dimmed the light in her eyes. For myself, because the ceaseless complaining and visits to the nursing home would come to an end. For five years, my mother-in-law was dependent on the care of strangers, and in the absence of a daughter, dependent on me to shop for clothing and personal items, none of which were ever quite right. I filled the role of stand-in daughter grudgingly.

Her death was not unexpected, and it *was* a relief, but the sadness and guilt I felt took me by surprise. Margaret had a fierce love for Catherine. Catherine described her grandmother as "eccentric" and found humour in her fussing and pleasure in the ways she showed her obvious pride. I'd never had the grace to extend my hand except when she needed it, nor to laugh in the moments that were truly funny.

Paul had long since made peace with the mother who, in his

childhood, had only a stout stick for dealing with her anger when the dithering patience failed. That, he said, had ended when he, barely into his teens, sat down with her and told her that he would be the "good boy" she wanted him to be if she put away the stick. As an adult, he generously acknowledged that, like all parents who fall short of the ideal, she did the best she could with what she had.

Paul had been raised Catholic but declared himself "done" in his teens. To Margaret's further distress, Catherine and I attended a Lutheran church. When Catherine was a baby, we wondered if Grandma would sneak her out to nearby St. Bridget's and have her baptized. Perhaps she had._All of that considered, I stayed out of the discussion about funeral arrangements, and apparently, it was so long since anyone else in the family had been practising the religion that they took their guidance from the priest. Margaret, he said, had been a devout Catholic woman, and we should assume that what she would have wanted was a traditional funeral Mass. When Paul said he would like to offer a few words about his mother, he was reminded that there is no place in the Requiem Mass for eulogies. So many rules. It seemed it was as hard to die a traditional Catholic as it was to live as one.

Because I knew Margaret loved music, when the choosing of hymns came up, no matter how hard I pressed my lips together, I felt sure I knew what she would have wanted. I mentioned some favourites I'd heard her sing while she puttered in her kitchen. Struck out again. No matter how much Margaret loved Marg and Charlie's rendering of "Abide with Me" on *Don Messer's Jubilee*, it was *a Protestant* hymn and therefore off limits.

At the beginning of the Mass, before the casket was brought to the front of the church, someone would drape it with a pure white cloth. A niece—with the right measure of piety—had already signed on for that task. This was a ritual that should surely have been Catherine's as the eldest granddaughter. In our family album, there is a snapshot of a little girl, barely a year old, in a flower-sprigged dress. Alone in the photo, she is taking a wobbly first step, but the hand she is clutching belongs to the grandma just outside the frame.

ONE MORE VISIT to the nursing home was required, one last clean-up.

Unlike the emptying of the house five years before, this job was easy. But wrenchingly sad. At the end of the bed, there was a faded afghan. Margaret had moved to the nursing home with this blanket wrapped around her shoulders. The afghan, a few photos, and my mother-in-law's rosary went into a small suitcase—Paul's decisions. The only garment I set aside was a silky, long-sleeved dress the colour of raspberry ice cream that she'd saved for special occasions. A closed casket, we'd told the funeral director, but still, Margaret would have wanted to look her best.

The handful of fabric I was holding felt as cold and lonely as the room with the stripped bed, barren bulletin board, and two green garbage bags at the door that held the clothing she had brought with her and was destined for the Thrift Store bin. The thought of her thin body in nothing but this icy breath of a dress was too much.

I grabbed Paul's arm. "What time is it?"

"Nine-thirty."

"We need to go shopping."

"For what?"

I danced the dress in front of him. "A warm sweater," I said. With only a breath of a pause, he nodded and grabbed the little suitcase, and we raced to the car.

We reached Wal-Mart fifteen minutes before closing time, dress in hand. Picked our way through racks of sweaters, me muttering, "Too flimsy, too slithery, too tacky, too drab." I sounded like Dr. Seuss. Paul finally took my arm. "This isn't working." He glanced at his watch. "What about the afghan?"

I let go of the sleeve of a white cardigan. Imagined a satin-lined casket, a silk dress. A shabby blanket? It was special to her and to Paul, because her beloved mother had crocheted it, but part of her ensemble for this special occasion? We agreed that it should be folded and placed at her feet.

And what about undergarments, stockings? How could I have imagined her laid to rest in nothing but a dress? I wish we had asked the undertaker what clothes they needed, but surely that choice should be ours. Hers. I scooped up a cotton slip, cotton panties, pantyhose. There were none of these in the dresser drawers at the nursing home. Nothing in her wardrobe but pyjamas, boxes of Depends, and the fleece pants and sweat-shirts I'd bought as endlessly as the harsh laundering at the facility wore them down.

A cheery voice announced that the store was closing.

Paul pointed across the aisle at another rack of sweaters. He took the dress from me, strode away, and randomly pulled out a hanger. "Does this match?"

Perfectly. A shade darker than the dress, a delicate lacy pattern and soft as a kitten. I held the sweater to my cheek, and then to his. She'd love it.

In the car, I put my head back and closed my eyes. Now I could envision Margaret in her gleaming mahogany casket. For thirty-five years, we had been connected in a relationship that neither of us truly understood. Therein lay the seed of my grief and my need to dress her up in the way she would have wanted. And as a wedding gift from Margaret, I would tell Catherine that I believe Grandma would have come to the celebration in her raspberry-coloured dress.

She would have worn the pearls.

KICK

JUSTIN DECIDES before he leaves the school at lunchtime that he's not going to tell his mom about Will. She'll find out soon enough. In the parking lot, he spies a rock with a good edge, about the size of a hacky sack. A sweet kick sends the stone flying down the street, Justin panting after it. He can hear Amanda calling behind him, but he ignores her.

When he opens the front door, he can smell fish and green onions. In the kitchen, his mom, still in her housecoat, shuffles from the fridge to the counter, mixing tuna for sandwiches. "Stinks in here," he says, and when she yawns, he asks, "Did you sleep?" She worked twelve-hour shifts all weekend, and now she has four days off. When Justin left for school, she was trying to decide whether to sleep or tough it out.

"Some," she says. She whacks a sandwich into quarters and slides the plate in front of him. "Remember this when I'm old. Any mom who got up out of her bed after three hours of sleep to make lunch for a fourteen-year-old deserves big boxes of chocolates in The Home."

She scrubs her hands under the tap like she's at work. She's a nurse, and Justin's sure their kitchen is clean enough for brain surgery. He picks the bits of green out of the sandwich, then makes a tower of the four pieces.

His mom pours a glass of milk, sets it in front of him. Musses his hair, and then wrinkles her nose. "You didn't shower this morning."

"Sure I did," he lies. His throat closes around the first bite of sandwich.

The same choky feeling as this morning when Mr. Waters stood in front of homeroom, blinking so fast it looked as though there were insects behind the lenses of his glasses. "Class, we have terrible news today."

Justin coughs the wad of sandwich into a napkin.

His mom watches his face for a minute and then puts her hand on his forehead. "What's up?"

"My throat feels funny." He glugs down half of the milk. "That's all I want." Swiping away the milk moustache with the back of his hand, he stands up. When she has that squinty look, she can read his mind. "I'd better go."

Still squinting, she asks, "Did something happen this morning?"

Oh, yeah. Something happened all right. He mumbles and stumbles through the stuff Mr. Waters told them. About Will and his mom and dad and his sisters in the van in California. And somebody came through that red light, and Will's dad couldn't stop.

"Oh my God, Justin!" She grabs him and pulls him so close he can feel her heart thumping like it's his own. His face is pressed to the nighttime smell of her housecoat. "How terrible for Will and his family! Are they okay? Was anyone else besides his dad hurt?"

He can't talk because of that taste in his mouth. She's got it wrong, but he doesn't correct her. He just shakes his head and pulls away. With the tips of her fingers between her lips, she looks like a little kid. He knows that as soon as he leaves the house, she'll flop down in the rocker in the living room and stare at the wall. He wishes he weren't going to walk out the door and leave her thinking Will's dad is dead. But she'll have a worse afternoon if she knows it's Will.

Halfway to school, still booting the rock, the inside of his foot starts to ache, a soft, mushy hurt like pressing on an old bruise. A glance at his watch, and he slows down so that he can time his arrival to the bell. There are clumps of Grade 8s standing around the door, girls crying and holding each other the way they did this morning.

Except for Amanda, who swoops down on him at the edge of the parking lot. She hooks her foot in front of his and lofts his rock onto the playing field. "Why didn't you wait for me, you dork? I was calling you." She's about four inches taller than he is this year. His mom says the boys will catch up in high school, that Justin will grow into his weight. But for now, he still feels like a blimp, which is why he goes home for lunch. He doesn't need anyone ragging him about stuffing his face. Amanda says she goes home because the girls in Grade 8 are airheads, and she doesn't want to hang out with them. She says she can't wait to go back up north for the summer.

Jason and Amanda have been friends since kindergarten. She and her mom live across the street with Amanda's grandparents. Every summer, Amanda spends a month in Yellowknife with her dad and her other grandmother. At the end of August, she comes back acting like some kind of junior shaman with a new supply of bones and feathers and other stuff her mom won't let her keep in their house. Most of it is in a box under Justin's bed.

They wait on the fringe.

"Sucks, huh?" she says. She's chewing on her thumbnail, looking away from Justin whenever he glances toward her. "Will's such a turd, but I never hoped he'd die."

Justin feels like she kicked him in the gut. Maybe she never hoped Will would die, but she has to know that Justin did. Every time Will yanked the toque off Justin's head and filled it with snow, snatched his backpack and threw it in the air, and all his pencils and homework tumbled into the wind; every time Will puffed out his cheeks and grinned and said, "Justin's got high cholesterol!" Every single time, he wished Will would drop dead. But there was always Amanda, helping him brush the snow off his stuff, stomping along beside him all the way home, shouting at him. "Justin, you have to be a bear! Nobody messes with Bear!"

Finally, the bell rings and they trail in together. They have math with Mr. Waters first period after lunch, so they go back to their home room.

Justin slides into his desk and looks straight ahead over top of the empty chair in front of him. Are they going to leave it there? Waters hands out a letter for parents. He says it's about the memorial service for Will. The math test on Thursday is postponed because he knows that some of the students will want to attend. Justin folds the letter and crams it into his pocket. Mr. Waters is still talking. "For those of you who were friends of Will's, there's a counsellor in the office this afternoon." He begins to point and call out names. And the first one out of his mouth is "Justin."

Friends? Does Waters think he's doing Justin a favour by including him? Amanda says thanks, but no thanks, when he calls her name. "I really didn't know him very well," she says.

Justin wishes he'd thought of that line, but more than anything, he wants to get out of the room, so he shuffles to the door with everyone else. In the hall, he waits until they're ahead of him, the girls whispering and sniffing, and then ducks into the washroom. Sits there on a toilet and watches the minutes click past on his wrist. He knows the routine with the counsellor. When his Grade 5 teacher's baby died, a counsellor came to the classroom. To help them "make sense of it," the principal said. Like there's any sense in babies dying. Justin already knew from his mom's job at the hospital that shitty things happen to kids.

After half an hour, he peeks down the hall. Through the glass wall in the office, he can see a few of his classmates waiting in the chairs. Girls. The ones who probably never even talked to Will. Finally, Justin slips back into the classroom, into his desk. Amanda is looking at him out of the corner of her eye.

He closes his eyes and tries to drown out the voices. Since morning, he's been afraid to think about Will. Afraid he'll see him all mangled and bloody. But instead, he's imagining Will in the chair in front of him. Will turning with that twisted grin, lifting a cheek, and polluting the air around Justin. Then, holding his nose, and just loud enough for everyone to hear, "Ewwwww. Justin! Silent but deadly!"

Justin gags. He swears he can smell the fart even though it's a dream. He gets up without telling Mr. Waters where he's going and runs for the washroom. After he spits into the sink, he rinses his mouth and then hides in a cubicle until the bell rings for the next class.

At dismissal, the hacky sack guys hang out in the stairwell. Sometimes, Justin spies on them from the top of the stairs after everyone else is gone. Pretends to be waiting for someone. Usually, they're playing "clock," and he fingers the knitted grey footbag in his pocket, knowing that he's better than any of them. A guy like Will—if he did normal stuff like hacky sack instead of following Justin around—would kick in and join them, all jokey. But Justin's not good at jokey, and he doesn't need anyone telling him to get lost. Today, he races ahead, wanting to be first out of the school. The rock is in the soccer field—one bounce from a Slurpee cup, exactly where he marked it in his mind.

Kick, kick, kick, takes him halfway home before Amanda catches up. "So, what did she tell you?"

Justin shrugs. Lines up the rock with his toe and wraps his fingers around the hacky sack in his pocket. The dense weave has a comfortable, scratchy feel.

"You didn't go, did you? I'll bet you sat in the can the whole time." After the kick, she races beside him. Amanda is the only person he knows who can talk in a normal voice when she's running full-out. "So, are you going to the funeral?"

He stops and bends over to catch his breath. "Are you?"

"I dunno," she says. "Maybe. If you go." Then Amanda turns and races ahead of him. From behind, it looks as though she's flying, one foot hardly back on the ground before the other rises. In front of her house, she waves without looking back.

His mom meets him at the door. Hands on his shoulders, she makes him look straight into her eyes. "Why didn't you tell me it was Will who died, not his dad? Oh, Justin, I would have let you stay home this afternoon. How sad. The two of you were such good friends when the family moved here."

Yeah. Good friends. When Will arrived halfway through Grade 6, the other guys cut him out. Justin already knew what it felt like to be alone, so he talked to Will at recess, and they started going to each other's houses to play video games. They even had sleepovers. But in Grade 7, Will started to make other friends and decided that having Justin as his pal kind of got in the way. He started scoring points by joining a crew of the other guys who never missed a chance to make Justin feel small. Then he led the way with his "high cholesterol" taunts, and so much more.

"I did tell you it was Will. But you misunderstood. I didn't want to talk about it, okay?" Her hands drift down his arms, squeeze his wrists and let go.

"Okay. I called the school. They said they had a counsellor talk to the class. How was that?"

He hates lying to her. Most of the time, he gets away with half the truth. "Stupid," he says. "They said it was for Will's friends, and Waters made me go."

"And...?"

"I didn't even like Will!"

"Oh. Oh, I see." She has that look on her face. Like she understands everything, but she doesn't. Not any of it. She heads for the couch now, leading him by the hand. "Sit down a minute."

Her eyes are shiny. She takes a Kleenex out of her pocket. There's a whole wad on the floor beside her chair. "Know why I'm crying?"

"Well, yeah. A kid died. It's sad."

"All afternoon I've been imagining how I'd feel if it were you. And feeling so glad that it wasn't. Because maybe if it were someone else's boy, then that means that particular tragedy is used up, and it can't happen around here again. Do you understand?"

Oh, jeez, same as when they're going to fly somewhere and she says she's relieved if there's already been a plane crash in the last few months because it decreases the chances. Statistics. And then she feels guilty for being glad that other people crashed. "Yeah," he says. He's tired, suddenly. He feels like putting his head on her shoulder. Instead, he pats her hand. And she smiles. "Guilt, right?" he asks. "You feel guilty."

"Uh-huh. How about you? Do you feel guilty because you didn't like Will, and now he's dead?"

"No," Justin says. "I feel guilty because I don't feel guilty." He's afraid for a minute that she'll think he's trying to be a smartass, but she keeps on nodding. He pulls the folded paper out of his pocket and hands it to her. His gut is rumbling. He'd like to grate some cheddar and make nachos.

She reads the letter and looks up at him. "I think we should go to this service."

"Maybe," he says. If he says no, the discussion will go on for much longer. She smooths the paper on her knee and looks thoughtful.

"You know, funerals are for making peace, Justin. Maybe you could go and just think about what you'd have said to Will if you'd known he was going on a trip and it would end this way."

Whoa! *Glad you're leaving, but sorry you're going to die, jerk?* Yeah, that sounds like something the counsellor lady would have suggested. Not.

His mom is frowning, waiting for him to answer. "Justin?"

"Yeah, sure. If we go, maybe I'll do that. Think about what I'd say to him."

"So, we'll go to the funeral."

"Maybe," he says. "If Amanda comes."

AMANDA, all in black, looks like a raven. Black pants, black sweater, and her black hair loose on her shoulders. She barges into Justin's bedroom on Thursday afternoon while he's changing from school clothes into his khakis and button shirt. Ten seconds before, he was tugging on the pants, zipping his fly. His shirt is unbuttoned, his feet bare. "Crap, Amanda! Can't you knock?"

She shrugs and spreads out on his bed, head on the pillow, arms wide. "I don't think we should go," she says.

"Well, it's too late. My mom won't back down now, and your grandma and your mom said they thought it was a good idea for you to come with us." The buttons seem too big for the holes. He works his way slowly to the bottom. When he looks up, Amanda is taking deep breaths and then exhaling as though she's going to die. "What are you doing?"

"Justin," she says in a squeaky voice that does not sound at all like Amanda, "I think I killed him."

"What?" He stares at her. "That's ridiculous. Their van got hit by another car. In California."

"I know," she whispers, "but I think I made it happen."

"Aw, man!" He can't take this. Not one of Amanda's visions. Not today.

She lurches up and swings her feet to the floor. "See, I made this amulet about a month ago."

"You put a curse on Will." His voice is as heavy as the stone in his stomach. "Amanda, that's kid stuff and you know it."

"I did not put a curse on anyone, you idiot. Shamanism is about communicating, not about evil spells. I made this amulet for you. To put you in touch with Bear. So that you would be strong and so Will would never bother you again. I think it may have backfired." She swoops down beside the bed and lifts the corner of the mattress. Her hand emerges holding a cloth bag. With her teeth, she rips open the stitching at one end and tumbles the contents onto the quilt.

Justin kneels beside the bed and picks through the two chicken bones, a clump of orange hair, and a tiny translucent claw. "You hid even more of this crap in my room?" He holds it between his thumb and first finger. "And this would be... The claw of the sacred grizzly?"

"Right. Symbolically. Actually, it's one of Dandy's claws." The clump of orange hair was obviously donated by Amanda's cat as well.

Justin stuffs the bits back into the little bag and hands it to her. "I don't want any amulets, Amanda. I just want to get this over with."

On the way to the funeral home, Justin's mom tells them it's not really a funeral but a memorial service. There won't be a casket. Amanda, who seems to have left her guilt in Justin's bedroom, chats with his mom about cremation versus burial. Justin refuses to have an opinion and stares out the window, wishing he'd been a bear instead of a rabbit when his mom suggested this.

When they park at the funeral home, he considers faking a sick stomach. Like that works when your mom is a nurse. He follows Amanda in black and his mom in her navy coat and high-heeled shoes into a lobby where clumps of people stand talking quietly. He can't spot any of the other guys from school, but Mr. Waters glides over to say he's proud of Justin for coming. Even Justin's mom can't think of a comeback to that one. Justin's already told his mom that the deal is they leave right after the service. No standing around after, no talking to Will's family. He figures the last thing Will's parents need is to see other kids today. Live kids.

On a table in front of the chapel door, there's a blown-up photo of Will in a baseball uniform. He's winding up to pitch with a look of intense concentration. Justin doesn't remember ever seeing that expression on Will's face. With the blue eyes and the blonde Afro like a huge halo under the baseball cap, Will looks like a kid in a Disney movie.

A sign with flowery writing says, "These were a few of his favourite things." Books: the whole *Black Stallion* series. DVD: *Happy Gilmore*. Pack of baseball cards. Bag of Doritos. Old acoustic guitar. Hacky sack, grey, with frayed threads. X-Box and disks for *Halo* and *Final Fantasy*.

He knows that *Final Fantasy* is his. He left it at Will's the last time they played together. Justin wants to turn and run. He feels like he's at his own funeral. These are a few of *his* favourite things, all things that he and Will shared.

Then the chapel doors open, and while they wait to file inside, Justin sees Amanda slip a rock onto the table. He absolutely is not going to ask her about it later.

The chapel is packed. They sit in the back row, which is not nearly far enough away from all those people who look like aunts and uncles and cousins at the front. There are at least two other kids with wild blonde hair like Will's. He wonders if they knew what Will was really like. He wonders if he knew.

Justin doesn't try to sing along, but his mom and Amanda are right into the program. They're both pretty awful singers. A few words from an uncle, then a man who was Will's baseball coach, then a minister talks, and then finally, Will's dad steps up and thanks them all for coming. He starts to say that he knows Will must be smiling down at this wonderful gathering... and then he chokes up and walks back to his seat, and the music begins for one last song.

While everyone else is making their way to the room with the coffee and trays of sweets, Justin's mom signs the guest book. Justin waits while she writes a message that uses up all the space beside their names and then runs down the margin of the page.

He knows that on the way home, she's going to ask him if he thought about it. About what he would have said to Will if he'd known he wasn't ever going to see him again.

Justin watches the murmuring guests in the reception room. Looks back at the kid in the picture on the table. At the plain grey hacky sack. A deep breath, and then he puts his shoulders back so that he feels much taller and walks through the doorway to stand in front of Will's mom. "I'm Justin," he says. "Will sat in front of me this year. And last year too."

The woman takes his hand and holds on tight. "Of course, I remember you. You were such a good friend to Will." Will's mom puts a wobbly smile on her face and turns to the person pressing up behind him. Amanda and his mom have followed him into the room, but he turns and leaves them there.

Outside in the parking lot, he squints in the bright sunlight. What would he have said? *Nothing*, he'll tell her.

But then he takes out his hacky sack. "Hey, Will," he whispers. "Wanna rally?" A couple of slow kicks, then heels and toes fly, and he dances on his little patch of funeral home pavement. When his mom and Amanda finally come out the door, the sack still hasn't hit the ground.

RAW

ERICA HAS NEVER BEEN able to sleep until Julian is home in his bed. She's been dozing and texting every hour. No reply. The damn bed is too big. The house is too quiet. She could have invited Warren to stay the night. He'd certainly hinted. When she looks at the pillow next to hers, she imagines Warren quietly slumbering. Would she wake him just to have him put his arms around her and tell her everything would be fine? She'd tell him to go back to sleep and she'd keep texting.

Instead, she'll wake Joe. He answers on the fourth ring. His voice is raspy and she's glad she dragged him out of sleep. Then he's mumbling before she has a chance to get a word in, and she knows he's talking to someone else. Someone in bed with him.

"I just want you to know that it's 4:00 AM and your son is not home, and he's not answering my texts."

"Erica." He clears his throat. "The kid is seventeen years old and he's not seriously into. booze or drugs. If he stays out overnight now and again there has to be a girl involved. Maybe this one is a hottie." She can almost hear him wink.

"Not seriously into booze or drugs? What do you know that I don't? I work in a school, Joe. Every kid is at risk where drugs are concerned."

"Come on. Imagine the worst thing that could have happened. He's dead, and you can't do anything about it, so get some sleep before the cops come."

"I might be able to imagine *you* dead," she says, "but never Julian."

"All right, all right. You know I'm joking." More whispering. "It's four o'clock in the morning."

"Right. That's why I'm calling."

"I have to get up in two hours. You're a mean woman, Erica."

At eight o'clock, Erica goes down the hall to Julian's room and stands in the doorway contemplating the empty bed. Forget texting. She'll phone his friends. For a couple of them, the boys she's known for years, she has only the landline and two of the mothers who answer run up to their sons' bedrooms to check. No. Only their own asleep, no overnight campers. Two cell phones go directly to voice mail, and groggy Peter stammers and stumbles and says he's pretty sure Julian fell asleep on the floor while they were playing *Call of Duty*.

Finally she phones Melissa, who is unlikely to have been playing a video game in someone's basement. Julian may have mentioned his plans to her at some point. Melissa calls often.

"He didn't come home last night?" Melissa squeaks. Erica has known Melissa since she was in kindergarten and knows that in Melissa's house the four kids write their destination, contact number, ETD and ETA on a whiteboard in the kitchen. When Julian told her and Joe about this, he was bug-eyed with disbelief. Joe shook his finger at Julian and told him not to be too sure of himself. Big Mother *was* watching. He winked at Erica.

"Erica, I've left text messages about studying together this morning and he doesn't answer. Could you please, please ask him to call me the minute he gets home? We have a big History test of Monday and he's not ready for it." A pause as though Melissa's gathering the words for her next sentence. "Could I talk to you sometime? Julian and I have always been close but lately . . ."

At 9:00 Warren calls. "Good morning, lovely lady. I hope I didn't wake you. I want to thank you again for last night. As always, the ending was especially sweet."

Sex on the sofa, the way their date nights usually end. When Warren first suggested they move to somewhere more comfortable, Erica played it coy. She's afraid they'll be so warm and comfy in her bed, they'll fall asleep and Warren and Julian will intersect in the kitchen in the morning. Erica hates the sound of her voice when she tries to do "coy." She knows Julian would nod, say good morning, and then ignore Warren.

It infuriates her that the indelible imprint of Joe's head is still on the pillow. So unfair to Warren. It's unlikely that Julian would tell his dad about the one time he came home early and walked in on his mom's "sweet ending" with Warren. She knows Joe would give her a rousing "You go, Girl!" the next time he stopped in, and she would tell him to go to hell.

In her angry ruminating, Erica's almost forgotten that there is a voice getting louder on her phone. "Erica? Are you still there? Good. Just wondering about tonight. Buddha's Kitchen still good for dinner? I haven't checked the movies, because you're better at choosing than I am."

"Buddha will be fine. Warren, could you please choose the movie this time?" She knows he's being kind, but his reluctance to "impose" his preferences in music, and films and so many of the other things couples do together gives her the sense that she doesn't really know this man. Except when it comes to food; at the first of their meals together, she saw him recoil when she cut into a dripping red piece of steak. He quickly explained that it was digestive issues that kept him on the vegetarian plan, not major moral or political objections to eating meat.

But how about the movie for tonight. "Honestly, Warren, I'd really like for us to see something you've had on your own list."

"Well," he said, "I have been watching some Netflix documentaries. I think you'd like *The Magical Andes*, which I just saw. Another on my list is David Attenborough's *Our Planet*." That one's on climate change." Of course it is. "Would you like to come here for a change? We can get take-out food and binge a bit on Netflix."

"That sounds like an alternative," she says, wondering how well it will segue into sofa sex. "Sure, it's about time we played in your sandbox." Dead silence. Ayiyi, Erica! Sounds like she's implying that his interests are childish? She laughs. "No, really, Warren. It will be a nice change from the Hollywood dramas I've dragged you to." The last movie they saw was *Ma Rainey's Black Bottom*, which Warren had declared a fine film, but she'd over-heard him telling someone in the staff room that while he appre-ciated the statement on racial injustice, he couldn't truly relate to the music and the characters. She'd chosen it because Julian had come home from Joe's saying that his dad was raving about the music and the characters. Julian was going to start listening to some of those old blues musicians. So he said.

"What time shall I come over?" she asks. He offers, as always, to pick her up and, as always, she tells him how kind he is, but she can get there under her own steam.

Erica has known Warren for years. They teach at the same school. About six months after Joe left, Warren gave her a shoulder to cry on and told her he'd always wanted to be more than a friend. He went from being a friend to being the kind of man a couple of friends told her they coveted. She'd hit the jackpot just as she deserved. So considerate. So generous. So reli-able. But lately, so predictable. So unlike Joe, whose crazy spon-taneity was like riding a wild wave.

She remembers a story about a couple in marriage coun-selling. When the therapist asked the wife what it was that most bothered her about her husband, she said it was the way he breathed. The problem with Warren, was that even in bed he scarcely made a sound. The silent lover made her self-conscious about her own moans of pleasure. Joe used to yip during coitus, and in sleep he snored like a hibernating grizzly.

Erica is standing at the window when a car pulls up and

Julian unfolds himself from the passenger seat. He waves and the car shoots away with a bleat of the horn, much too fast on this quiet street. As he lopes toward the house, Erica is struck by how much Julian looks like Joe now that he's not a scrawny kid anymore.

"Sorry, Mom," he says on his way in the door. "We went over to Kyle's after practice and played video games and I totally lost track of the time until it was way too late to phone and I didn't want to wake you." He finally exhales.

"Wake me? Julian, are you not aware that I don't sleep until you get home? Why do you think I always meet you at the door? Don't tell me you were trying to be considerate. This kind of thing is damn well inconsiderate and irresponsible."

"Irresponsible how?"

"You keep me awake imagining the worst. Sleep? I don't want to go to the door all groggy in my housecoat when the police come." She knows that doesn't make sense if Julian is really listening. "Accidents happen, and of course that's the first thing on my mind."

"I'm seventeen, Mom. I'm moving to Toronto to go to school in the fall. If you don't trust me now, are you going to worry about me unless I phone you every night so you can sing me to sleep?"

Not only is he looking more and more like Joe, he's sounding like him too. She takes a deep breath and lets the sarcasm go. "Who drove you home?"

"Just a friend. No one you've met."

"Friends don't have names anymore?"

"Sure," he says, his back to her as he heads for the stairs. "That was Taylor." Despite the non-gender-specific name, Erica knows this is the "hottie" Joe was imagining.

"Taylor spent the night at Kyle's too?" He slams the bedroom door behind him.

She goes halfway up the stairs to shout. "Melissa called," she lies. "She says you have a date to study for a big exam."

She needs coffee. The new coffee maker on the counter is a birthday gift from Warren. He was appalled the first time he saw her battered espresso pot. It only looked bad, she told him, because they took it along on camping trips and used it over an open fire. Makes great coffee. She didn't tell him that she and Joe had a custody battle over the pot when Joe left, and she kept it hidden in the freezer for a whole year. Warren suggested she give it away now that she has a decent machine.

Not a chance. She wants a tiny cupful of rich black caffeine. She's tired of the milky lattes Warren picks up for her on the way to school. She's never mentioned a love of lattes. She likes her coffee black. Erica shoves the Cuisinart into the corner, pulls the espresso pot out of the cupboard, and slams it onto the stove. She dumps three scoops of the coffee Warren likes into the pot. She'll buy a fresh bag of her favourite coffee beans tomorrow. But it will need to be ground, because when Joe stormed around and couldn't find the pot, he grabbed the grinder on his way out.

The first sip of coffee scalds her tongue. The second tastes bitter. Joe likes his coffee with raw sugar, and she finds the can in the spot where the pot and grinder used to live. She pours a few brown crystals into her hand and licks them off her palm. The sweetness crunches between her teeth. Julian might need a hit of caffeine if Melissa shows up to study. She checks the fridge to see if there's something for the kid to eat. She needs to make a run to the grocery store but isn't going there today. Nope. Tonight she's probably having Thai food—a frequent choice with options for both the carnivore and the vegetarian.

Warren. Erica knows that she's hanging onto him for the wrong reasons. When it began, she was so very lonely and relieved that there was a man who found her attractive. Then there was the hope they'd run into Joe, and she'd hook her arm through Warren's and pull him tight to her hip. That did happen once, and Joe gave Warren a hearty clap on the back and told him it was great to meet him.

Who wouldn't warm to this nice man who wants a good

woman on the pillow next to him for the rest of their lives? And that, she decides, is what he deserves and why she needs to call him back and tell him she's not the one.

"About tonight," she says, when he answers on the first ring, so cheerful. "I'm sorry, Warren, but I can't go out with you."

A pause, then he sounds as though he's taken a step closer to her by pressing the phone tight to his ear. "Something's come up?" he asks. "Do you want to postpone? How about tomorrow night?"

She hears Julian's door open, his bare feet padding down the stairs. She takes the phone into the living room. Julian pauses at the bottom of the stairs, and then veers left into the kitchen.

"I don't think so. Warren, I'm terribly sorry, but I don't think this is working. Us, I mean."

"When did you decide this?" Warren asks. "I don't understand, Erica. Why don't you come over tonight, and we can talk."

Erica hears the ping of the microwave. "There's no point in giving it another try," she says. "I'm afraid I'll still end up hurting you." She's standing at the window, the dry heat of the furnace blowing the sheer curtains, blowing into her face. She doesn't know what she expected, really, but she's surprised when Warren doesn't press.

"All right then," he says. "All the best, Erica."

And he's gone. She stares at the dead phone in her hand. Easy? Then why the small door that's just opened in her chest. And the feeling that she's looking into an empty room.

Mom?" Julian has come around the corner with a platter of nachos. "That sounded like a break-up," he says. "You want to talk about it?" He sounds uncertain, his mother's boyfriend uncharted territory. The only comment he's ever made was that Warren didn't seem her type.

"Not now. But thanks, Julian." she says "Maybe later. Go have your nap."

"I can't," he says. "Melissa wants to come over and study."

He puts the platter on the coffee table, flops down on the sofa and stares at the ceiling. "I have a bit of a problem here, Mom."

Erica feels a kick in her chest. "What's that?" she asks, lifting his feet so she can sit and hold them on her lap. She puts her head back and stares at the ceiling too. There's a scar in the stipple from one of the books she launched the night Joe came out of the bedroom with a backpack and said he was leaving.

Julian raises himself onto his elbows and pulls a couple of pillows under his back so that he looks comfortably reclined now. "See, there's this girl, Taylor, I told you about?" He reaches for a clump of nachos and stuffs them into his mouth.

"Barely," she says.

"Yeah well, I really like her." He chomps away at the cheesy mess in his mouth and looks at Erica as though she's the one standing in the way of a relationship with Taylor.

"But there's Melissa," she says.

"Yeah, and that's the problem."

"The problem is that you don't want to go steady with Melissa anymore, and how do you get out of that?"

He groans. "Going steady?"

As with many other things, she doesn't know the teen vernacular. "Okay, whatever you call this friendship you and Melissa have had for umpteen years, and that seems to me pretty serious."

"That's the thing, though. It's not serious to me and I don't want it to be exclusive."

"So you still want to see Melissa?

"Well sure, like friends."

"And when you told her that, she said . . . ?"

He loops his arms under his head. "I haven't actually told her yet. I was thinking I'd send her a text."

"Julian!"

"Well you just blew off Whatshisname in a phone call."

"Right," she says, "and I feel shitty about doing that." She grasps his ankles and scowls at him. "If you're sure this is what you want, then tell Melissa. Not a text! What? I heart you but, and then a sad emoji?

Julian shrugs. "Maybe it would be better to just wait and see how it goes with Taylor?"

Erica looks up at that rent in the stipple. She's supposed to know what to say here. There is no answer on the ceiling. "You know what, Julian? Why don't you talk to your dad about this? He seems to consider himself an expert."

"I already did."

"And what did he say?"

"He said you're way smarter and I should ask you."

Damn right, she is. "Listen Julian, I'm an expert in what it feels like when someone you love packs up his toothbrush and a change of clothes and says that maybe he'll be back. Gradually, you notice that his stuff has been disappearing but he doesn't have the guts to come and get it while you're home."

Julian is staring at her. "Mom . . . I don't get what this has to do with me and Melissa. You're talking about Dad, right."

"Figure it out. Do what you want." Erica throws Julian's feet on the floor and leaves him lying there.

She picks an apple out of the bowl in the kitchen. She sinks her teeth into the crisp flesh, stands at the window and watches a flock of waxwings ravage the berries on the mountain ash.

Julian goes back to his room and closes the door. A few minutes later he calls down to tell her that he made the phone call. He's sure that in a couple of weeks Melissa will be okay with the break. He's going out with Taylor later tonight. So no studying, but she knows he won't fail the exam. As for Melissa, she'll ace it.

Erica opens the fridge again. She and Julian will have burgers. Big fat burgers. She takes out a package of ground beef, rips off the plastic and thunks it into a bowl. She cracks an egg onto the meat, a handful of breadcrumbs, salt and pepper, then sinks in her fingers and kneads the fleshy mess, her hands aching from the cold.

Without thinking, she pinches off a small knob of hamburger and pops it into her mouth. Joe said that the first time he saw her do this, he went weak in the knees. He growled when he grabbed her and pressed his mouth to hers, his tongue frantic for the raw meat. Erica braces her hands on the counter and breathes until the wave of longing passes. She spits the pasty glob of meat into the sink.

YOU MUST REMEMBER THAT

HANK FLITTED in and out of Lillian's dreams all night. Even though it's her long-ago Hank, the sweet man she married, who comes to her, she awakes feeling restless.

Five years of haunting her. She doesn't feel guilty for wanting him asleep in the grave.

If only the frigid air mass would lift so she could go for a calming walk.

By the time she finishes her coffee and toast, Hank is at her again. Dreamy Hank has slipped away to where all the comforting ghosts go. Miserable Hank is back.

You stay inside, Lillian. One slip on those sidewalks, you'll break a hip, and from there, it's all downhill.

She knows the slippery slopes, the worst one being the decline that turned Hank into a stranger.

The day wears on into the afternoon, and the nagging never ceases. Lillian tries hard to pretend she can't hear Hank. She wants to remind him of the advice they learned in one of the foster parent sessions on communication. *Do not ever begin a sentence with "You should!"*

The phone rings, likely Carol calling to say goodnight.

Calling to check up on her. "Still alive," she answers every time. Then, "Just on my way to bed."

But it isn't Carol. Lillian thinks the man says his name is Rob. There's a lot of static—bad reception on this little flip phone Carol bought for her. She's to keep it beside her at all times in case of an emergency. Sometimes, Carol sounds too much like her dad.

Damn right. She's a smart girl, our Carol. But how the hell did this guy get the number?

Lil tunes Hank out, strains to hear the voice on the other end of the phone. He apologizes for calling so late. It's just past 9 p.m. "I wonder if you remember me."

Remember someone whose voice she doesn't recognize and whose name she barely heard? Probably not a salesman, though, not with that line. "I'm sorry," she says. "You'll have to give me a clue."

"I was one of your foster kids, long time ago."

Hang up, Lillian! If he is one of those kids, he wants something from you.

Twenty-five years of looking after those sad, sweet children.

Sweet? Yeah, in the beginning, we got the sweet ones, but remember how it worked out in the end?

It seems a lifetime ago. She used to pride herself on remembering her foster children, but these days, the young faces swim in a mist in her memory. The photo albums that take up a whole shelf in the bookcase help when someone comes to mind. Rob? When did they have a Rob? There's a Bobby she remembers well; he was with them the longest, one of Hank's favourites. She hasn't heard from many of them since they moved on.

And a good thing, too! For Chrissake, Lil, with those older kids, I knew some of them were heading in the wrong direction when they left here. Tell this guy he's got the wrong number, the wrong Aunty Lil.

"I was just passing through, and thought I'd give you a call. Still living in the same house, eh?"

How could he have remembered the house well enough to

find his way back? Hank did everything he could to block their phone number and address when they stopped fostering.

I wanted some control over who turned up at our door.

Internet? It seems nothing is private these days.

Should she pretend to remember? "How old are you now, Rob?" she asks, trying to get a handle on him. Count back to when this man was still a boy, to the period in their lives when they cared for him.

"Thirty this year," he says.

Lillian goes into the living room to the photo albums. She mutes the television on her way past. She only keeps it on for the voices that add some life to the house.

"Are you busy?" he wants to know.

Busy? Until the phone call, she'd been sitting at the kitchen table since she finished her bowl of stew, drinking coffee, arguing in her head with Hank.

Lil, you should not be living alone. You promised me you'd move.

She shakes her head. It was only to give him some peace of mind at the time.

"Aunty Lil?"

The little ones called her Mommy, the older ones, Aunty Lil. Hank was never Daddy, just Uncle Hank. "Yes, I'm here."

She pulls one of the albums off the shelf and sits down in her chair. The book is labelled HOLIDAYS #2. She can usually find a child in all the years of Easter, Halloween, and Christmas photos. There's another album labelled SCHOOL PICTURES with those mug shots from the beginning of each year, but it's not as reliable. So many of her kids missed picture day.

"I'm only in town for a couple of days. Can I stop in?"

For God's sake, Lillian, tell him you're busy and hang up the phone.

She flips pages. Here's Bobby hanging tinsel on the tree. He lives out at the coast now and sends a card every Christmas. How many Robs or Bobs could there have been?

"Hello?" Foster Rob is shouting into the phone.

"Yes, yes," she says. "I'm here." Two more pages and there's

Robbie, Halloween 1991. The boy in the cowboy suit could be thirty by now. Yes, she decides, this must be Cowboy Robbie calling.

Could also be in jail if he's one we didn't keep for long. Maybe just got out.

"Yeah, but are you busy? Do you have time for a visit?"

At nine o'clock at night? Tell him you don't visit after six o'clock. Or better yet, tell him your calendar is full.

"I'm not busy." When is she ever busy these days? Twenty years ago, she would have given her right foot for two hours of this solitude.

Peter Mansbridge used to be the finishing touch to each boring day. Good news, bad news, at least his calm voice helped her to believe the world was still a safe place. Now they've replaced him with a gaggle of others, and the news keeps getting worse. She goes to bed before *The National*, and prays that, in the night, Hank will drift away into eternal life. Somewhere else.

She's turning pages in the album but has forgotten what she's looking for. Robbie. He wants to talk with her. "Robbie? Where are you?"

"In front of your house."

She slides the album onto the coffee table and walks to the window with the phone. Under the skeleton branches of a cottonwood poplar, a man stands hunched into his jacket. Ice fog hangs a halo around the streetlamp. "Well, for heaven's sake. It's cold out there. Come on in."

Lillian!

She goes back to the table, takes one more look at the picture, and closes the album. She can see him coming up the walk now.

Look what you've done!

They'll sit here in the living room with the television muted. She'll serve coffee and ask about his life, and when the cups are empty, she'll say she's tired. How good of him to remember her. He'll write his address in her book, and next month she'll send a Christmas card.

When she opens the door, there is nothing in the face of the gaunt man with the wispy moustache that evokes the child. There are deep lines carved around his nose and his mouth, grooves in his forehead like steps ascending high into the receding hair. He extends a hand crusted with calluses. "Aunty Lil. Long time, eh?"

She steps aside to let him in, catches a whiff of stale cigarette. He stops just inside the door and makes a labour of undoing the snaps on the skimpy jacket. A cell phone pokes out of his pocket, and a patch below the right shoulder says he works for a trucking company.

Unless he stole the coat. Maybe the phone too.

Jacket in hand, Robbie steps out of his running shoes, toe to heel like a child. He grins at her, showing a row of higgledy-piggledy teeth.

"Only place I ever lived where you had to leave your shoes at the door," he says. "Bet you're surprised I remember that?"

Lillian shakes her head. Where did he fit in, this man-child whose memory of her house rules makes him less of a stranger? "I hope you remember some other things I taught you." One of the girls who came back to visit said it was because of Lillian's training that she never leaves the house, not for anything, without peeing first.

He turns toward the kitchen, but Lillian takes the jacket from him, hangs it on the coat rack, and motions to the living room.

"You go sit down. I'll bring us a cup of coffee." He looks like he could use a bowl of stew, only there's nothing left in the pot but gravy and a few pieces of vegetables. She doesn't have any cookies. *Crackers and cheese will be fine,* she thinks.

"I can't drink coffee," he says. He winces and rubs the front of the greying t-shirt just above his belt. There are tiny holes in the fabric as though it's been shot with sand. "Stomach trouble."

She feels a tweak of recognition; a child doubled over at the back door, not wanting to go to school. Stomach ache, the whiney voice pleading. But it could have been any one of several children.

"How about a glass of juice?" she says.

Now you've got it. Keep it simple, make it quick. Eat, drink, put the empty cup down, and it's time to go.

"Juice?" He laughs. "Nah, just a glass of water."

Back and forth from the fridge to the tray on the table, she watches him through the kitchen door.

Robbie circles the room, picking up everything movable; each one of her mother's Hummel figurines on the mantelpiece, photos on top of the piano. Swirls the peppermints in the candy dish on the television with his finger. Stops finally in front of the bookcase and stands there squinting at the framed certificate on the wall while she carries the snack into the room.

He flicks his fingers at the award. "Foster Parents of the Year?"

"That was quite a while back," she tells him. "Before Hank got sick. You know Hank died?"

So far, he hasn't asked about me at all.

"Too bad." Robbie shrugs. "I guess he was pretty old when I lived here. A lot older than you, eh?"

Lillian bites her lip, feels like looking over her shoulder. Hank hated that people thought he was older. She motions to the couch and sits down, but Robbie paces. When the cell phone on the coffee table rings, she reaches for it and then pulls her hand back. "They'll leave a message. It's likely Carol. She checks in every evening to make sure I'm still alive." She smiles, but he simply stares back at her.

Answer it! At least tell Carol you've let in some old foster kid, and if she doesn't hear from you in half an hour, she'd better get her ass over here.

"You remember our daughter, Carol? Our youngest?"

"Right. You had a couple of real kids of your own. Was Carol the one who played the piano?" He finally sits down beside her. He's wearing heavy work socks, but his feet look small. "I remember sneaking in here a couple of times and trying to make some music. Until the time the old man came in and slammed the cover down over the keys. Lucky I got my fingers out fast."

Oh, no. He was one of the last. "Do you still like music?"

"I'd like to have a piano someday," Robbie says. There is such a change in his voice, such earnestness in the way he looks straight at her, nodding, his feet splayed on her living room rug.

Tell him he should buy a dental plan before he buys that piano.

"Are you married, Robbie?" she asks. "Any children?"

"Sure," he says. "We've got two kids. Boy and a girl."

Too fast. Any answer that comes back that fast is a lie.

"Where do you live? Next time, you should bring the family."

"You know how it is," he says. "They're busy with stuff. School and like that."

He drinks the water in three quick gulps, puts the glass on the table, and swipes his wrist across his mouth. His arms look ropy, stronger than the rest of him. Lillian passes the plate, but he shakes his head. "I can't eat cheese."

She nods. "Oh, yes. I remember now." She doesn't, really, but so many of her kids had digestive problems. These days, it seems everyone has trouble with wheat or milk or peanuts. With the album across her knees, she flips it open and turns it so it's facing him. "Look at this," she says. It's a photo of Hank with his arms around a small boy, teaching him how to hold a baseball bat, and another of Hank holding onto the back of a bike with a little girl poised to pedal. Then Hank, with the baseball teams he coached, sometimes two or three of the foster kids in uniform.

Robbie sucks his teeth. "I don't remember any of that."

Lil flips another page to "Halloween," and a couple of princesses and a pirate. She turns the album in his direction. "We had so much fun with costumes."

Robbie looks around the silent room. "This place feels smaller than I remember."

"And to me it feels bigger," Lil says. "All the empty beds."

She's flipped a few more pages in the album, looking for the little cowboy. "You must remember this Halloween. Look at the smile on your face?"

He squints at the photo and then stabs at the name under it. "What the hell? Is that why you keep calling me Robbie? That's not me. My name is Robert."

He starts to pull the album away, and for a few seconds she resists, and they're caught in a tug-of-war.

I told you! I told you!

When she lets go, he pulls the book onto his own lap, hunches forward, and begins turning pages. Lillian clasps her hands to keep them from shaking.

Two, three, four pages later, he taps on the plastic covering. "I remember that kid. Darla, right? She peed the bed every night, and the stinkin' sheet was always in the bathtub in the morning."

Lillian nods. She tries to take a deep breath, but her chest hurts. She watches the credits roll on the quiet television screen. Robert. Yes, of course. He and Darla were here at the same time. The last two foster children. Almost twenty years ago. A photo of Darla, but none of Robert. Lil raises her eyes. She knows Hank is still here, and she knows he remembers. But he's silent.

Robert, not Robbie, was away visiting with his mother the weekend they discovered that there was some money missing. When the social worker brought him back and they told her about the money, she made Robert empty his pockets, and there was no fistful of change, just bills. More than had gone missing from the sugar bowl.

Robert insisted his mom's boyfriend gave him the money. Hank insisted the social worker pack up Robert's clothes immediately. He would not abide a little liar, he said.

That was a problem? I was protecting the home. Our home!

Robert is standing now, circling the room again. He smacks his fist into the palm of his hand.

"Robert, you and Darla were the last two," Lil says. "Hank

was sick. We couldn't take in any more children." They weren't *allowed* to take any more foster children. Hank had become "erratic," was how they put it.

It's clear now. Robert was only with them for a few months. There were others who had come and gone just before he arrived. They've never come back. Not one of those other shadowy children, including Darla, would ever come back.

"Sick?" He's behind the couch now, and she has to turn her head and look up to see his face. "He was a freakin' maniac. Just good old Uncle Hank in the morning, and a screaming nutcase if we didn't sit up straight at the table at suppertime."

"Please sit down, Robert. Tell me where you went from here?" Her voice quavers.

"I don't think you need to know, so let's just say I moved around. Back with my mom on and off." He lifts the album to sit down again, lets his hands go slack on top of the photos.

"Well, now, that's good to hear. How is your mom?" She clasps her hands to keep them from trembling.

"I haven't got a clue." He slams the album shut, thumps it onto the table. He stares at her. "You're scared of me."

"Of course not." Lillian shakes her head.

"Yeah, you are," he says. "You think I'd hurt you?"

"No, Robert. I know you wouldn't do that." She takes a long, slow breath, then another. The tension in her chest eases slightly. "But it's getting late." How long since he came? She is tired, not sleepy, that heavy weariness that pins you down like bags of sand.

"Yeah, I'm going, but first I'll tell you why I really came back. I remembered you all these years, the nice aunty who told me I was going to stay with you, no more foster homes. I was like ten years old, and you were the best. But Hank. That guy was a real shit, if you'll pardon my language. I was afraid of him, even though he never hurt me. He was the other kind of mean."

"Oh, Robert." Lillian is remembering a scrawny little boy now, with a quivering lip and eyes that came close but never spilled tears. She remembers gathering him onto her lap. She remembers his clothes. They were packed into a garbage bag. The children always came with those black garbage bags of belongings. Mostly, they left with decent suitcases, but Robbie left with garbage bags. "Hank was sick. The kind of sick that turned him into somebody I scarcely knew by the time he died."

"Yeah. I get it. But you never stuck up for me. Not about the money, or the way he looked at me like I was something stuck on the bottom of his shoe. Know why I came here? See, I didn't know he was dead, and I was going to get right in his face and tell the bastard he was wrong."

Lillian has fallen back on the sofa and can only shake and shake her head. "I'm so sorry, Robert. Truly, I am. Hank's sickness was in his mind. He was such a good man when he was young, but as he got older..."

When Robbie stands, he seems to tower over her. He bangs his shin on the edge of the coffee table as he turns toward the door, swears under his breath. "Just a minute," Lillian says, and pushes out of her seat. She takes her wallet out of the drawer in the table in the hall. She is waiting to hear Hank's voice tell her to just get the man out of there as fast as she can, but not a whisper.

At the front door, she fumbles out two ten-dollar bills. It's all she has.

Halfway into the nylon jacket, he pushes away her hand with his elbow. "I don't want your damn money. You think that's why I came? To beat you up and steal your money?"

"No, no, Robert. I'm glad you came, glad things are going well for you," she says. "Buy something for your children."

A sound like air escaping a tire puffs from his lips. He takes a step back, lifts his chin, and looks her in the eye. "I lived with a woman for a while," he says. "We had a kid. I guess he'd be about eight now."

"Well, then, take it for him," Lillian says. "Put it in a card and send it to your little boy from his Aunty Lil." She slips the bills into his pocket. "Please?"

"Whatever. It'll buy some of the gas to get out of this town." Finally, he nods and finishes snapping up the fasteners on the jacket.

Lillian. The sugar bowl. His voice is calm, no shouting.

"Wait!" she holds up her hand and runs to the kitchen. There's fifty dollars in the bowl.

Robert turns up his collar, opens the door. A gust of sleet slams it shut.

"Here. We don't want you running short on your way home." She's afraid to think about where home might be. This time, he takes the money without hesitating.

See, I told you he needed something. But now Hank's voice is barely a whisper in her mind.

She holds out her hand. Robert hesitates a moment before he offers his. She covers it with her other hand, and he looks her in the eye and nods before he pulls away. Then he turns and steps quickly down the sidewalk. Out to the street.

Lillian closes the door, stands for a minute, then yanks it open again. "You come back again, Robert!" she calls. "You know where to find me."

But he's already too far away to hear.

JEWEL

BARBARA DIDN'T TELL Gary she was going to visit his Aunt Jewel. He'd want to know why, and Barbara doesn't know the answer to that question.

But here she is, pulling open the first set of doors at the entrance to Woodcrest— wondering why so many nursing homes and seniors' residences, even posh ones, pretend to be in the woods, and why there are always Adirondack chairs on the lawn—and there's a woman clumping toward her in a walker. There's no one behind the woman, no one in sight at all. Barbara hesitates. Should she help this patient out the door?

"Relax," the woman tells her. "I'm as *compos mentis* as you are." She presses a button on the wall and the exit whooshes open. Outside, she settles into one of the big wooden chairs and lights up a cigarette. Barbara wonders how she'll ever get out of that chair again, never mind back inside. Perhaps she *should* alert a staff member. On the other hand, the woman made it outside on her own and hasn't set off any alarms. And for the money people pay for this place surely someone is watching.

Inside, Barbara hesitates. There's no one at the reception desk. So many corridors. She doesn't remember which one she and Gary followed when they dropped in with a plate of shortbread last Christmas. Or maybe it was two Christmases ago. One thing Barbara hasn't forgotten is the smell; not even the cloying perfume of two vases of lilies at the reception desk and the reek of disinfectant can mask the underlying fecal scent. Barbara wishes she had a less sensitive nose. She wishes she'd taken a deeper breath before she stepped inside.

A woman finally appears at the reception desk and tells Barbara that Jewel has moved up to the second floor. She says it with a lilt, as though Jewel strode out of her room and punched that elevator button all on her own. Barbara has been in enough care facilities to know that upward mobility is about loss of mobility. Why hasn't someone in the family mentioned that Jewel is losing it?

Jewel is sitting in a wheelchair at the window, her chin resting on her chest. Barbara hesitates in the doorway, and coughs ever so quietly. Jewel's head snaps up, and she squints.

For no reason whatsoever and to her embarrassment, Barb waves as though she's just spotted someone familiar in a passing car. "Hel-lo Aunt Jewel! It's me, Barbara, Gary's wife. Your nephew Gary?"

"I know who Gary is." It wasn't loss of voice that precipitated the move upstairs. Jewel sounds testy. Aunt Jewel, the spinster teacher, the family's legendary lesbian.

"Bullshit," Gary always insisted. "Gossip. Just because she never married. Maybe she wanted to be a history professor instead of a housewife."

"Some people," Barbara reminded him, "do both." She herself has been a teacher *and* a mother.

"Not in Jewel's day," he said. "Gossip."

Choice pieces of Jewel's furniture from home followed her to the care facility, followed her upstairs. Dark mahogany desk still waxed to a shine, pens in a brass cup, small stack of envelopes neatly squared on a leather-cornered blotter.

Jewel interrupts Barbara's snoopy scan of the room to ask

what brings her here. Her voice is still strong, but the lines on her forehead deepen.

"A bit of family news," Barbara says. "I don't know if anyone has told you our Kaitlyn is getting married next month." She moves out of the doorway and walks to stand beside Jewel's wheelchair. Who would have told her? And why? "To her roommate at Ryerson —Diana," Barbara says. "Kaitlyn and Diana are getting married."

In her mind she whispers, like you and Henrietta, but Barbara never knew Henrietta. Henrietta, who Jewel called "Hank." This Barbara gleaned from Gary's sister who is the source of all she knows of Jewel and Henrietta / Hank who is part of the legend of Jewel the lesbian. How they roomed together at McGill. Stayed close after they graduated in spite of the miles between them. The teaching positions, Jewel in Edmonton, Henrietta in Montreal. Visits back and forth at Christmas, and every summer vacation together. A new picture of the two of them in London, Rome, Madrid, in Jewel's Christmas cards.

Until suddenly no Henrietta, no more mention of Hank. None, and no one dared to ask. "She'd bite your head off," Gary's sister told Barbara. Briefly, rumours of another woman, another professor colleague, but only Jewel's smart solo presence at family functions ever after.

Jewel was likely described as handsome in her youth. Her steel grey hair is cut Prince Valiant style across a broad forehead, and she's dressed in a tweed skirt and pale pink sweater, leather walking shoes on her feet, solid on the floor. The deep-set hoods of her eyes droop, but only for a second until she peers out from under the lids. "It's legal now? For women to marry women?"

"The law just passed," Barbara says, as breathless as though she hauled a tablet carved with Bill C-38 to the top of the mountain herself.

"Is that so?" Jewel closes her eyes. Her chin sags. Now Barbara sees the drip-drip stains on the sweater, the snag in the hem of the skirt, and wonders who looks after Jewel's clothes.

Who provides the personal touch? There are no grown daughters, just gossipy nieces wary of this aged aunt.

A woman in a floral print uniform glides into the room with a tray in her hands, eyes flashing into every corner. This is the one who should be watching the smoker out front. "How lovely! You have company," she chirps. She plants a hand on Jewel's shoulder. Jewel's eyes open. The woman hands Jewel a tiny paper cup and a glass of water.

Jewel swallows the pills and crumples the cup. "I know I have company," she says.

Just when Barbara has decided that now the news has been shared, she can leave any time, the nurse shifts a chair into position, beckons Barbara into it facing Jewel, their knees touching. "There you go."

"Gary will be happy to pick you up for the wedding," Barbara tells Aunt Jewel. Gary is going to be furious.

"I do not go out these days," Jewel says. Clear voice, clear eyes, clear as can be. "I got your news when the invitation came in the mail." But a minute later, she sighs and drifts away again.

Sounds of squeaky feet in the hallway, rattling, the whine of something hydraulic; a lift for someone else who's up here because they're down? Barbara fidgets, leans forward in her chair, elbows on her knees, and chin in her hands. Now *she* sighs. It must be the air in this place.

The invitation, Gary told her, was just formality, wedding protocol. "You're probably wondering why I've come, then," she says. Not a twitch from Jewel. "Oh, I don't know." Barbara sighs again. "I'm good with this wedding, and the relationship. Things are so different these days. So open."

"Not like it was for you and Henrietta," she whispers to herself. "Not how I imagined Kaitlyn's life." Oh, she hopes it was a whisper.

Jewel's head bobs up a notch, her mouth opens, a soft snore creeps out. Jewel is asleep. "It's a good thing that it's all open now, don't you think? I'm fine with it. Only . . . it's like when I sing inside my head, you know? I'm Joan Baez in my mind. In real life, when the song pours out of my mouth I'm off-key. When I try to tell people about this wedding, I see the way they smile, and I can't sing the song I want to sing. I don't know the words nor the melody. Why is that?" she says softly. She waits, wanting Jewel to show signs of . . . Barbara isn't sure. Gladness that the law has passed? Offer assurances that this is exactly as it should be? Anger that it took so damned long and Jewel and Hank might have . . . ?

Jewel stirs, her tongue working against her teeth. Barbara dares to reach for a knotted hand, surprised by the softness of the skin. She strokes the map of veins with her fingertips. "I'm sorry," she tells Jewel. "I shouldn't have come. I can't seem to get any of this right." She gently releases the hand to rest in the folds of tweed across Jewel's knees. "I'll let you rest. But Gary and I will come again soon." A lie and an unnecessary one. Jewel won't want to see the wedding pictures.

When Barbara has moved her chair back against the wall and turns to say goodbye, Jewel's eyes are open wide and clear. "Henrietta got married, you know. To a man." Hands clenching the wooden arms of the chair, she pulls up straight, her head high. "Oh, don't look so sad. It was long ago. These things happen."

She looks straight into Barbara's eyes. "Don't worry. You'll get it right."

PARTY FAVOURS

I WANTED to go to the park. I wanted to sit on a bench in the sun and watch children fly to the moon on the swings and give each other "bumps" on the teeter-totter. That was the finish I wanted for this spring day.

Amy wanted a playmate. "The park's no fun if Megan can't come."

"Megan's not your only friend. Maybe someone else will be there."

I held Amy's running shoes out, but she crossed her arms and scrunched her narrow shoulders up around her ears. She looked like a sad little sparrow that had fledged too soon. "Phone Loretta again," she said.

I would not call again. There had been something in Loretta's, "Megan isn't home." Not quite apologetic, but short on details.

"Daddy's going to be home soon with pizza. Let's go quickly, just you and me. Moms need exercise, you know." And a blessed change of scenery.

Motherhood. I'd imagined busy days full of noise and toys that ended with two sleepy children tucked into their beds to make way for adult time. Not so naïve as to buy into the television version of the perfect family, but not expecting to raise an only child. Shouldn't it be easier, just one child?

I dropped Amy's shoes in front of the door and pointed at them. She shook her head. When Megan outgrew the shoes and Loretta handed them down to us, Amy loved them. Because they'd been Megan's. Now they were scuffed and worn. We'd just bought a pair of pink-and-white striped runners a half size too big. They would fit perfectly by fall. New school shoes in September.

All the other girls in Amy's class wore shoes two sizes larger than hers. Most of the girls were a head taller than Amy. Given the awesome cognitive levels Amy had achieved, the neonatal gurus had assured us that before long, she would catch up in size as well. Meanwhile, we had a tiny bright little girl who didn't feel small. She considered every child she knew to be a friend.

"But I want to play with Megan," she said. I knelt down, put my hands on her shoulders and looked into those dark blue eyes. They were going to spill. At this time of day, Amy's eyes couldn't blink fast enough to hold back tears.

I stood up, reached into the closet for the shoe box, lifted the new shoes out of the crinkly tissue, and dangled them in front of her. "Want to try these out, just once for play?" The day was sunny, the ground was dry, and maybe, just maybe, pretty shoes could set it right.

"Yes!" She took the shoes from my hand, sat down on the floor, and slid her feet into them. She pulled the Velcro tab across, pressed it down, then up—zip!—then across again and up and zip. I thought it was as much the sound as the colour of those shoes that thrilled her. Velcro. Marvellous invention. But how were we meant to teach our children to tie?

The play lot was deserted; swings hanging dead straight, one tiny striped sock stuffed through a link in the fence. Amy ran up the aluminum slope of the slide, the new shoes giving her super-power traction. At the top, she spread her arms and grinned at me, then turned in a tight circle to look at the fence that enclosed Megan's backyard.

Oh, be careful, be careful. I still caught myself holding my breath when Amy looked as though she was trying to balance on the head of a pin. She was agile, the fall was short, and the sand was deep. *Relax, relax, relax.*

I looked away from the slide toward the sound of someone approaching. There was Loretta, pushing the stroller in the direction of home. Her boy was asleep, head lolling on his shoulder. "Have time to sit for a few minutes?" I called.

"Love to, but I'm not taking a chance on this little dude waking up." Loretta waved and kept on walking.

"Hey!" Amy called after them. "I could come to your house and wait for Megan to get home."

Loretta turned. "Not today, honey. Too close to suppertime."

Amy came down the slide on her belly and dangled off the end, her fingers trailing circles in the sand.

"Do you want me to spin you on the merry-go-round?"

She shook her head.

"How about under-pushes on the swings? Really big ones!"

No again. "I want to go home now." She kicked at the sand with her new shoes. "These are good. We don't need to try them out anymore."

Amy chose the shortcut home, out into the alley and down the walkway that took us to our corner. Loretta was on the curb, peering down the length of the block. The stroller was parked on the lawn, baby still sleeping.

Amy tugged at my hand. If we were going home, we were going home. She wanted Megan, not Loretta. I pulled back, my eyes on a car that had turned the corner and was headed toward us. The station wagon cruised to a stop. All the windows were down; little girls were packed into the car, sputtering and giggling and sucking on candy sticks. Seven little girls, six of them watching Amy, but the one beside the driver concentrating on the green stick of candy in her hand.

Amy, the eighth little girl in the Grade 1 class, standing on the sidewalk in her pretty new shoes. She blinked and blinked and held tight to my hand.

Megan bounced out of the car. "Thanks! Mini-golf was so fun!" The paper bag in her hand was covered in red crayoned hearts. The goodie bag. Party swag. Loot: shiny baubles, Happy Birthday pencils, stickers, candy in cellophane bags tied up with pink ribbons.

When the car pulled away, Amy waved.

Megan held up the loot bag. "Look! Gummy bears and a Barbie necklace!"

Loretta grabbed Megan's arm. "We have to go in and make supper. Say goodbye to Amy."

Megan stared at her mom's red face, then at Amy's face and mine, then down at her feet. "Oh. Yeah. Hi, Amy." A crooked little smile, then, "Bye, Amy."

On the short walk home, Amy skipped across the breaks in the sidewalk. Step on a crack, break your mother's back.

"Let's sit out here for a minute." I pulled her close to me on the front step. "Did you know it was Brianna's birthday?"

"She gave out the party cards at school. She told me she couldn't invite me because her mom said she could only have six girls. Because she's turning seven, you know? And with six girls and her, that makes seven? Is that a birthday rule?"

"No. That is not a birthday rule. We would never leave out a friend, would we?"

She shook her head.

When Jack arrived with the pizza a half hour later, Amy was in her room, rummaging in the box of junk in the corner, and then into the pantry and back to her room. I knew so well what his reaction would be that I almost didn't tell him about this time, this one more instance of being left outside the circle.

"The bitch!"

"Who? Brianna or her mom?"

"Both of them. I don't want that kid in this house ever again."

I didn't remind him that Amy's birthday was coming up in July. We had no rule of six plus the birthday girl makes seven.

When I called Amy to the table, she danced out of her room with a brown paper bag.

"What's that?"

"It's loot, Daddy!" She emptied the bag onto her plate: a juice box, a ring with a purple stone from the dentist's office, a tiny plastic unicorn, a serving-size box of Froot Loops, and a scrap of pink cloth. Barbie's scarf.

Loretta would make sure that Megan phoned tomorrow.

We would go to the park.

What else could I do?

BOX SOCIAL

IT WAS A STRANGE TIME. Locked down because of the COVID-19 virus, nowhere to go, nothing to look forward to, I found myself looking backward. I dreamed about people and places I hadn't thought about in decades. Back and back, younger and younger, to a time when I was an awkward ten-year-old in a new school, and a boy named Reinhardt sat at the back of the class.

IN OCTOBER, a month into the school year, I was "the new kid" in a Grade 4 classroom with more than twice as many students as the school I had left. From a small town where everyone knew me, I'd come to a small city where my mom and dad knew half a dozen people.

The pleading of a ten-year-old didn't make a ripple in the discussion about the move. If I'd been a kicker and a screamer, my parents might have heard me. Maybe even listened. As it was, I got Mom's lecture on being a quiet child—a good thing—as opposed to a timid child who missed out on things she would have enjoyed. How, I wanted to know, was I supposed to stop being timid?

Mom dressed me in my Sunday clothes—a scratchy blue plaid skirt and a white blouse with a Peter Pan collar. Like all my clothes, these were stitched on her Singer machine, and always with some "room to grow." Then she marched me down to the elementary school just two blocks from home. Oh, but it looked big, that square two-storey brick building.

Once she'd delivered me to the principal's office, Mom left. No, she told the principal, she could wait to meet my new teacher another time. I knew what she was up to—throwing me in the deep end, assuming the pep talk she'd given me about my "shyness" was sufficient to give me water wings.

When the principal ushered me into the classroom, I might as well have been on stage in an auditorium. The thirty-two faces and everything about and around them were a blur.

Mom had canvassed our street for someone my age and found Rose, who was also in Grade 4. I'd spent an hour in Rose's bedroom listening to her show-and-tell about her collection of Dolls of the World. The German doll looked like the picture of Gretel in my book of fairy tales: Hansel and Gretel in a hut in the forest with their poor woodcutter father. There had to be a wicked stepmother and a witch, because in all the stories, there were either poor kids or princesses, in which case, there had to be a prince.

While I'd been admiring Gretel's dirndl, my mom and Rose's had coffee together in the kitchen.

Rose raised her hand just as far as her chin and waved at me. The teacher, Miss McKenna, was all gushy about what a fine group of students I was joining and how she was sure they'd make me welcome.

I didn't want a welcome. What timid kid wants that kind of attention? I was already counting down the time until I could follow the breadcrumbs back home.

When everyone was concentrating on their arithmetic work-sheets, I raised my eyes to scan the rows ahead of me. I was dressed to fit in; no shortage of Peter Pan collars, but none that I could see with a signature touch like the blue rickrack with which my mom had embellished mine.

When the recess bell rang, I hung back; if I dawdled long enough, maybe everyone would be doing whatever they did at recess, and I could slip out and try to melt into the brick wall. I was sure Rose's mother, and likely mine as well, had told her to make sure the new girl didn't feel like a new girl.

Rose and three of her friends were waiting for me outside the door.

I let the names of the other three fly right past me; there were so many Kathys and Lindas and Barbaras and Donnas my age that I knew they were probably on that popular names list, and I'd forget who was who before we went back inside.

"I love your blouse," one of the girls said, and reached out and touched the zigzag on my collar with the tip of her finger. "Did somebody make it for you?" I let one shoulder twitch in a sort of shrug, and then shook my head. Not exactly a lie?

"Who cares?" Rose said. "Want to play Double Dutch?" She waggled two long skipping ropes in front of me. I had enough trouble skipping "Teddy Bear, Turn Around" with one rope without tripping. No way was I going to look like an idiot trying to skip between two ropes. I couldn't throw or catch like the kids on the ballfield either. A small group of girls were playing hopscotch. That, I could have handled.

"I'm not good at Double Dutch, but I can turn."

When we stepped away from the wall, I noticed someone in a corner where the walls met the protruding doorway. He had less chance than I did of being invisible. This was a very large boy who'd made an even slower exit than I did when the recess bell set us free.

Rose gave her end of the ropes a tug. "He doesn't want anyone to look at him. That's Reinhardt."

"Didn't you notice him when you came into the classroom?" one of the other girls asked. "He's hard to miss." She ballooned out her cheeks.

"He's one of the kids who come on the bus," Rose said.

A bus at a city school?

Rose pointed in the direction of the hopscotch game. "They're farm kids. They kind of keep to themselves."

I thought about the farm kids and the town kids I'd left behind and suddenly missed them terribly. The only difference had been that the farm kids ate at school —some lucky enough to have kits with Roy Rogers, or Lassie or Cinderella decals— and we town kids had to go home for chicken noodle soup from a can.

"They're not mean or anything. If you went over and asked if you could play, they'd let you," Rose said.

One of the KathyLindaBarbaras waved away the idea. "What's the point of making friends with people you only see during school?"

The school bus students, I found out later that day, had a separate lunchroom. If any of the town kids had to bring a lunch, they ate in the classroom. When the bell rang at the end of the day, there was a race to the bus. No shouting and waving goodbye.

When we went in after recess, Reinhardt was already there, at the back of the room. He looked like an obese, sun-burned farmer with the face of a boy. He wore men's overalls, the legs shortened for the height of a ten-year-old boy, and a flannel shirt. He had thick black hair, shaggy except for the unmistakable bowl shape across the top of his brow.

From my very first days in that Grade 4 class, I cringed at the loud whispers about his clothes, his size, the pinching of noses and moaning about the smell of garlic when he opened his lunch box. When he was called on in class, Reinhardt mumbled his response to the top of a table where he sat on a chair because he was too big for the desks.

I wanted him to look up. I could hear my mother's voice telling me to "Speak up! You have a voice." I knew, though, that Reinhardt was not trying to hide my kind of shyness. I didn't know the word "humiliation" at the time, but I did know the taunts were cruel.

Miss McKenna? Occasionally, she'd glance up from her desk and call out a sharp, "Class!" And then she went back to whatever she was marking.

Only once did I see someone on the playground stand beside Reinhardt. On a winter day, one of the boys ran past and tried to grab the winter hat with ear flaps that Reinhardt was wearing. A girl ran over, planted herself two feet away from the boy, and spit at him. "Leave him be!" She rattled off a string of German words; if I repeated them at home, I'd have been sent to the bathroom to wash out my mouth. For the kids who had never heard German spoken, the guttural language, the spit, and the look on the girl's face were enough.

She walked to the wall, leaned in, and whispered something to Reinhardt. Then she snarled at everyone else and walked away. Reinhardt went inside even though the bell hadn't rung. I wondered if he had an indoor hideaway as well.

"That's his sister!" Rose hissed.

The hat-bully, spit-upon boy would never tell on anyone, Rose said, because that would make him look like a sissy.

After school that day, I sought out my dad. I had questions, and I knew my mom would brush them away, but Dad would listen. He introduced me to the meaning of "scapegoat." He reminded me as well that although no one but Reinhardt's sister —and I'd only seen her that one time—came to his defence, I could be sure there were others who hated the bullying.

"They're a German farm community just east of the city. The people in this town are mainly English or Swedish or Norwegian, and even though it's been fifteen years since the last war with Germany ended and most of those farmers were in Canada before it even began, it takes a long time to forget."

"But we're German, and nobody's mean to us," I stammered.

He knelt down to my eye level. "Most people aren't aware that Becker is a German name. That boy you just mentioned, would that be one of the Muellers—a big boy with shabby clothes? The dad buys tires from me, and sometimes the son is with him."

I nodded. "His name is Reinhardt. They're awful to him. Even some of the German kids. If other kids hate how he's treated, why don't they say something?"

He cupped my face in his hands. "It's because that person would just get picked on too."

I nodded. I understood, but I was glad that I was Joyce, and not Gretel or Bridget.

IN FEBRUARY, Miss McKenna announced that rather than have a Valentine's party, our class was going to have a real old-fashioned box social. She was practically dancing on her toes with excitement. "Girls, you will all pack an extra special lunch for two. Everyone is staying for lunch that day; those of you who usually go home, and, of course, the bused students as well. We'll all be dining in the classroom."

Dining?

Miss McKenna said she had a letter for us to take home to our parents that would explain the party. This, she said, would replace her usual letter saying that every student was to bring a Valentine for every other student. No playing favourites, because that was how feelings were hurt.

"Isn't it lucky we have the same number of boys as we do girls? I'll put the names of the boys in this bowl, and you girls will come up, draw out a name, and off you go to share your lunch. Won't that be fun?"

There were groans, mainly from the boys. "Why can't we have a regular Valentine's party like everyone else?"

"No, no, no," Miss McKenna said. This was meant to be part of our studies as well as fun: there were box socials in the pioneer times we'd been learning about.

My mother shook her head. "That's going to turn sour," she predicted. "And she's got it wrong, too. Back in those 'olden days' she's talking about, this was an adult thing. The women decorated their lunchboxes, and the men bid on them. It was a way to make money for some needy cause or other."

In spite of all that, I noticed that she gave me a pretty fine lunch that day. No way was anyone going to be disappointed about sharing ham sandwiches, chocolate cupcakes, and grapes with her girl.

Up and up and up we went, pulling names from the bowl. Only five of us were left when Rose dipped her hand in, glanced at the slip of paper, burst into tears, and ran out of the room.

"Just carry on until everyone has a partner," Miss McKenna said. She followed Rose and came back into the dead quiet of the classroom after what was likely five minutes but seemed like an hour. She had her arm around Rose, who was still sniffling back tears.

"Reinhardt, please come up so Rose can share her lunch. Bring your chair with you." It was neither kind encouragement nor a firm request.

We all turned to look at the boy, who must have gone to the cloak room to get his working man's lunch kit. He was eating, head down as always. He looked up for just seconds and shook his head.

Rose was invited to sit at the front and have lunch with Miss McKenna.

I shared with a boy, who, to my relief, munched away in silence.

On the walk home from school, I was as quiet as usual—but so was Rose. She stopped in front of her house and turned to me. "I know that wasn't very nice, but how would you like to have lunch with Reinhardt?"

Ten other girls had hugged Rose and fussed over what a dreadful thing it would have been to sit at the back of the room at Reinhardt's table.

I shrugged and shook my head, and watched her walk into the house.

My dad posed a question that was different but the same when I told him and Mom the story at the supper table. "Which one did you feel sorry for? Rose or the boy?"

"Both, I guess."

In April, Reinhardt stopped coming to school, and his table and chair were gone.

A PLACE and people from more than sixty years ago. Just children. I didn't keep in touch with anyone after Mom died and Dad and I moved again, but when the memory of the box social surfaced, it came with vivid images of Rose's flight and Reinhardt's quiet presence at the back of the classroom.

I wanted to believe that Reinhardt had taken over the family farm, made a success of it, married, and raised some kids.

In a simple Google search, I found Reinhardt's obituary. He died at the age of sixty-four, eight years ago. No eulogy. No wife and children mentioned; survived by a brother and a sister; predeceased by parents and two other siblings. I couldn't find any information about the brother, but Canada 411 gave me the sister, Gladys Fleck. Address and phone number.

Phone? Where would I begin and what reason would I give for raking up the past? In fact, why did I feel the need to right something that it was unlikely anyone else remembered? A letter? How could I fill a page? I didn't have enough words.

I found a card. Heavy white stock—no image, no message inside.

Dear Gladys Fleck,

In 1958, I attended elementary school with your brother, Reinhardt. In the past few months, he has come to my mind often. Even

*so many years later, I can't help but be filled with shame and
sadness about the bullying he received at school.*

*Why am I writing to you? To tell you that I am sorry I was too
timid to stand up for Reinhardt.*

I sealed and mailed the letter. I didn't expect a response. But
a month later, a reply.

*I don't remember you. Neither would Reinhardt. He never
talked at home any more than at school. Don't blame yourself. That
was his life until he died, and there's nothing you could have done.
But thanks for remembering him. No one else does.*

Gladys

JAWBREAKER

MY GREAT-GRANDSON COMES FLYING through the back door and lands on me in a hug. He has a black-rimmed mouth, and the menu from his lunch is painted on his cheeks and chin and the front of his grey hoodie: ketchup and mustard and smears of grease.

"Here!" The contents of the white bag he's holding spill onto my lap. "Happy birthday!" Looks like Candy City is still in business, and Shane and Dakota have been shopping.

I'm tired, and not just because I'm eighty years old today. I'm tired because I've been watching Dakota's mom, my granddaughter, Karin, pace, and I am oh so tired of her husband at the kitchen table, who just a minute ago looked up from the newspaper to say yet again, "I've got this, Karin. It's going to stop."

I want to ignore him, but I have the sick feeling that what he's trying to stop are Dakota's visits with his birth father. Then I remind myself that there is a custody agreement that must surely have visiting rights spelled out.

Shane has stopped just inside the back door and sends me an airborne high five. "Yo! Irene. Happy birthday."

I return the high five. Karin hasn't acknowledged Shane's

presence but is fussing over the kid. "Dakota! Don't get that stuff all over GeeGee."

Where is my free-spirited granddaughter whom I never imagined worrying about a bag of candy? Nor did I ever imagine her married to someone so rigidly unlike the father of her child.

When Shane first appeared on the scene, older than Karin and she besotted with him, everyone was in high dudgeon, except me. I'd liked this man with the quick laugh and flashing eyes. Now they all felt she'd been rescued. Except me.

"It's not toxic, Karin," I say. I kiss Dakota's sticky cheek. "GeeGee loves it." The pants of my tracksuit are sugared with jelly beans, powdered fruit slices, pastel hearts with sweet words, and humbugs and chicken bones. "These sweets were called penny candy when you could buy something for a penny." Not likely Dakota has ever seen a penny.

Dakota flicks his tongue in and out. "Guess what makes your tongue go sicko black?"

I spy the black marbles in the pile. "Jawbreakers. One of my favourites."

Damn the weariness, I'm glad to have this red-cheeked great-grandson wiping black drool on the hem of my shirt. With Karin's parents—my daughter and son-in-law—snowbirding in Florida, I'd hoped my eightieth birthday would slide by with just a phone call and a card or two.

Then Karin called to tell me Dakota wanted a party for his GeeGee, and I could hear the little guy's "Please, please, please," in the background. I said I'd think about it.

For a decision involving a small boy, Rock Paper Scissors with my cat seemed like a good way to go. Clarence won. I knew all along he'd be rock.

Dakota reaches into the bag and pops a humbug into his mouth. "Shane said you like this kind of candy because it's old. Like you."

I raise my eyebrows at Shane. He shrugs, and his lips twitch with just the smallest of smiles.

Karin's man at the table—Rich, that's his name—turns in his chair to look at Shane. "Are you going to pay the dental bills for the sacks of sugar you feed him every time you take him out? Let's get on with it and do this cake. Dakota should be in bed by now."

Dakota slides off my lap and plants himself between the two men, his lower lip in a pout. "It is not bedtime. It's cake time." He glares at his mom. "Me and GeeGee love candy, and GeeGee loves her present."

No one ever asked me what title I wanted conferred on my status when Dakota was born. I've wondered how "Great One" would have gone over. One of my friends was given that crown after a lot of wine-drinking at her great-granddaughter's christening.

Karin moves to put her arms around Dakota, the two of them caught between birth father and stepfather. I've wondered what her life would have been if she'd stayed with Shane. They were living together in a small apartment above his friend's autobody shop. The parents were apoplectic. Leaving home to "shack up" with a guy who was picking up construction work wherever he could find it? Not the future they envisioned for their bright girl, who in a few months would have been university-bound.

There is a cold wind blowing into the kitchen from the open door. Shane finally pulls it closed. "You want me to go, Karin? I only came in to wish Irene a happy birthday."

"You can stay for cake if you want to," she says.

The cake on the counter has so much floral decoration, it's like a hat from a royal wedding. There's a solitary fat pink candle blooming with the roses.

"Sure. I got time for Irene's birthday."

I'm struck by how much Dakota looks like his father. Baby Dakota was a long, thin infant, with scarcely any cuddly baby fat. Now, at five, he isn't conventionally cute, but he's a kid who seems to bounce rather than walk, and fly rather than run.

Shane is tall, but no longer the skinny stretch of a man he was. He's muscular and confident and has the same flash in his dark eyes. He was mature, she told the parents, not like the other boys who buzzed around her. And he told her he loved how smart she was, and how proud he was going to be, no matter what she decided to do.

Pregnancy was clearly not something Karin had decided to do. They were being careful, she insisted. A month before the baby was due, she came home to stay. She was scared, she said. She didn't know what to do with a baby, and Shane had even less of a clue.

When it came to a toss-up between living above the autobody shop and a suite in her parents' basement and a car of her own, the rebellious streak peeled off like a dirty Band-Aid.

As relieved as I was that Karin was in a safe place, I'd felt a twinge of regret. I'd never been frightened for Karin because after I first met him, I didn't have the sense that Shane was a danger. I'd glimpsed signs of a risk-taker in my granddaughter, and I still dreamed about the times I'd ventured off the pavement and could have gone down some mossy paths. Regrets? Oh yes, I'd had a few.

Karin lights a match, sets the candle ablaze, and marches the flickering garden over to me.

Dakota reminds me to make a wish, and he blows the candle out in a giant puff. "What did you wish for, GeeGee?"

I shake my head. "You know that birthday wishes are secret, right?"

He sighs. "Yeah, but I really want to know yours."

My wish? That tomorrow, before I leave, I'll have the gumption to speak my mind to Karin about this nastiness to Shane. *But what would be the point?* I think as I share my cake with Dakota. His grandparents will be back soon, and they keep a firm grip on the wheel. Once I'm home in Victoria, what I don't know won't keep me awake at night.

Dakota is licking the plate when Karin pulls it away. She lifts Dakota from my knee and turns him toward the hallway, toward his room. "Away you go now and get your pyjamas on. I'll be there in a few minutes to read you a story."

"But... " Dakota stammers. "GeeGee has to read my story."

"GeeGee is tired," Karin says before I can tell him I'll be there in a minute. "She needs to get to bed, just like you."

"Yes, GeeGee is tired, sweetheart." So very tired. "But I'm not letting you get away without saying goodbye."

"A big 'mongous kiss, right? And a hug to hold me tight?"

"You bet!" I hold my arms wide and squeeze this boy close.

"And Daddy! I need to say goodbye to Daddy." Dakota runs to Shane and holds tight to his blue jean leg. "Remember what you promised." He tilts his head, and Shane nods down at him.

I see Karin glance at Whatshisname and then raise her eyebrows at Shane. I wonder what that was about, but keep my silence. I'm not getting involved. Karin, hands on hips, sighs when Dakota flies back to me. He leans close to whisper in my ear.

"Me and Shane have a secret," he whispers. "But I can't tell."

"No," I whisper back to him, "you mustn't tell." This tension I've been feeling is secrets. The room is a swirl of secrets.

When Dakota trudges down the hall, I see Shane rub his eyes. Time to go. For both of us.

Finally, I'm buttoning my coat at the door, trying not to breathe heavily, because Whatshisname has put on his jacket and is already holding my arm. He will insist on steering me to the car like a wood-footed dance partner he can't wait to be rid of.

"I can drive you," Shane says. "Where do you need to go?"

"My hotel's downtown. That would be good, Shane. Saves anyone else going out."

Although his hand lingers, I can feel Rich's relief at being divested of this duty. He steps aside.

After Karin has hugged me and whispered, "Thanks for coming, Gran, it means so much," we're finally out the door.

Shane doesn't hook himself to my arm. He lopes ahead and hauls open the door of his big black truck. "You want some help climbing in there?"

I don't hesitate to let Shane give me a boost. I like the way I'm sitting high in the seat. How long has it been since I rode in a truck? When Shane gets in the other side, I pat the dash. "I've always liked trucks."

We're still backing out of the driveway when Shane says, "What's up with the hotel, Irene? I remember you sleeping with Dakota when he was really small."

"The man says it's not appropriate for a boy to share his bed with his old GeeGee. And the spare bedroom is an office now." I don't need to tell him whose office it is. Rich offered the sofa bed in a basement bedroom, but my old bones shrieked at the very thought.

"I hope he's at least paying for the hotel," Shane says.

I'd made the reservation, and it hadn't occurred to me that there could have, should have, been an offer to pay. "You know me, Shane. I'm an independent old crow." He laughs. "But tell me what you're up to these days.

"Roofing."

"Must be getting cold up there."

"It's steady enough money that I can shut down if it's real bad," he says. "I work on my own, and I've got a good name."

"Good for you." I imagine him, agile on a rooftop, his hair tied back.

Shane pulls into the visitor parking. He turns off the truck and takes the key out of the ignition. "How about I walk in with you?"

Why not? "How about a cup of tea?" I've been feeling dry in the mouth since the birthday cake.

He nods. "Sure. I'd like that. I won't stay long."

"Don't worry. It might be bedtime for Dakota, but not for this old lady."

In the room, I pour water into the little coffee maker next to the bar fridge and drop tea bags into two cups.

Shane sits at a small table next to the window and drums his fingers on the tabletop. "I want to ask you something."

I shrug and raise my eyebrows.

"What do you do when your kid thinks you're his uncle? Dakota told me today that he's supposed to call me Uncle Shane instead of Daddy."

I pour the water—as hot as it's going to get—into mugs and put one on the table beside Shane, the string on the tea bag hanging over the rim. Then I sit on the edge of the bed, cup on the bedside table, bag of candy in my lap.

Shane is waiting for an answer to the question I've evaded. What *do* you do?

I pop one of the jawbreakers Dakota shared with me into my mouth and suck for a moment to give myself time to find the words. "I might tell him I'm still his dad, not his uncle, and I'll always be his dad?"

Shane just grunts. "There's more going on than this uncle talk. Did you hear about plans to cut me off from the kid?"

I sip the tea. It's tepid. I could honestly say that I hadn't heard a thing, but keep remembering Rich telling Karin that things were going to change. I just shake my head.

Shane is watching me, waiting for more. "See, this is why I need your help." He strains forward in the chair. "Ever since Karin hooked up with Jackass, you're the only one I trust in that family. I used to trust Karin, but she's different now."

Another moment of delay to brush the spilled sugar from the candy bag off the bedspread. "Shane, you and Karin have a custody agreement, do you not?"

Shane swats away my words like little gnats buzzing between us. "Yeah, it's down on paper, and Karin said she wants Dakota to know me."

I raise my arms. Praying for a little help? "Shane, it's so plain to me that Dakota loves you and loves spending time with you."

Shane speaks louder, the way some people do when they're talking to old women and aren't sure if the message is getting through. "You mean Karin didn't tell you anything about how that limp prick of a husband of hers...?" He stops and throws his head back. "Sorry about the language, but they got someone following me, not just when I have Dakota, but when I'm on my own doing what I do."

A small tremor sets the tea in my cup sloshing. I put it down.

"They want me out of the picture, Irene. They want to prove I'm a lousy father and Dakota isn't safe with me."

"Oh, Shane, that can't be so. Karin would not do that."

"You think she doesn't have a clue that someone's been tailing me the last three times I had the kid? Too bad that on one of those times, I made the mistake of leaving him in the truck for five minutes while I went into the liquor store to pick up some beer. I could see Dakota through the window the whole time, for Chrissake."

"Well, that was stupid." I can't help myself.

"Yeah, but I didn't think it was a big deal. We've all done something like that."

"But a liquor store, Shane. Couldn't you have waited until you'd taken Dakota home?"

"I didn't think it was a big deal until I saw the guy taking the picture. That's when I knew they were following me."

"They took a picture," I say.

"Yeah, they took a picture. They flashed it in my face when they started working out a new visiting plan today." Shane sits forward and presses his hands so hard into the arms of the chair, I can feel an ache in my arthritic fingers. He looks bigger than he did in Karin's kitchen. He's begun to grow and fill up the space in the small room.

I shake my head. "One picture doesn't make you a bad father." Unless there were other pictures.

"Look, would you just help me?"

"How? Shane, I have no influence in this family."

"Aren't you the great-grandmother?"

Yes, I am. The Great One with a shabby crown who chose to live in a faraway kingdom.

Louder still. "What if one of these times we're even later than usual? What if me and Dakota take a little trip? Sleep in a tent, roast hot dogs. He told me he'd like that." *Me and Shane have a secret,* Dakota had whispered.

The set of his jaw, the narrowing of his eyes—defiant, a different Shane.

"Why are you telling me this?" I ask.

"Maybe I thought you'd get it? Maybe I don't mean any of it, but I wanted somebody to know how it feels?"

I hate the quiver in my voice. "Yes, I can imagine how it feels, but you listen to me. I've always thought you were a good man. Think about the boy and how confusing this is already. If you take off with him, you'll make things even worse."

My throat is so tight I can't swallow. I grab a tissue and spit the jawbreaker into it. "I'm old, Shane. It upsets me to hear this."

The awkward silence that follows creates a barrier between me and Shane that I've never felt before. He must see the fear in my eyes.

"Well, I'm really sorry I troubled you, Irene." He stands up and zips his jacket high under his chin. A brief hesitation before he sticks out his hand.

I lay my own on top of his. "I have arthritis. My fingers will hurt if we shake hands."

From the window, I watch the black truck leave the parking lot.

Stretched out on the bed, heart pounding, I tell myself to make a wish. Just make a wish.

Sadly, I've never believed that wishes come true.

THE KEY

MAGGIE'S THUMB punched through the egg when she cracked it. Shattered bits of shell slithered into the milk along with the broken yoke. Liquid ingredients, dry ingredients... she was only trying to make muffins, for gawdsake. She poured the contents of the bowl into the compost pail. There was a bakery five minutes away. Diabetic muffins? Probably not.

This was how the day had gone. Two students in her Grade 8 homeroom running out in tears, a whole posse of other girls chasing after them into the washrooms. Temperature dropping from a sunny fifteen degrees to five, and a forecast of freezing rain by the time she left school. Text from Ron saying he had to work late.

But tomorrow was Saturday, and Joy was coming for coffee and a bitch session. In the shitstorm of today, Maggie had forgotten to confirm their date, but was sure that if there was a problem, Joy would have called.

Joy had told Maggie on Tuesday that she had a migraine. Predictable, she'd said. Barometer falling, hormones rising, full moon, all the usual stuff that messed with her head. Add a meeting with Kurt scheduled for Wednesday to finally sign the damn divorce papers, and the pain hit the ceiling of her skull.

Maggie wondered how the meeting had gone. Then, as though Maggie had conjured the man, the phone rang. "Do you still have the key to our house?" Kurt. Joy's ex-husband.

"Whose house?"

Kurt ignored the question. "When Joy and I put in the security system, we gave you a backup key. I don't have one anymore."

Liar. It was Joy's house. That much had already been inked onto the papers. But Kurt still had piles of his stuff there. When Joy wasn't home, he popped in and out and took what he fancied.

This Maggie knew because Joy had called last week to rant about the missing Keurig. The new woman must be a tea drinker, Joy said, or her condo just wasn't furnished to Kurt's comfort.

"I've been trying to get hold of Joy since yesterday. She didn't answer my texts. She's not answering today either."

Not surprising. Maggie remembered that Joy never answered texts or the phone if she knew it was Kurt calling. Even less surprising if she'd had an ugly meeting with him the day before. "Why don't you just go over and ring the bell?"

"That's why I'm calling *you*." He must be desperate if he was stooping to talk to her. "I'm here now. She's not answering the door."

Joy had likely gone out for TGIF happy hour with the work crowd, but she never stayed long. She liked to leave, she said, before she was the only sober one at the party.

"Sit on the step. I'm sure she'll be home any time now."

"Her car is in the driveway, but the house is dark."

Maggie sat down hard on a kitchen chair. On Tuesday, Joy had said she was going to the pharmacy on her way home from work and then to bed. *Lots to talk about over coffee on Saturday. Your place, right? I don't own a coffee machine anymore.*

"Maggie? Are you there?" Kurt was agitated.

I'll sleep this off. I'm meeting Kurt at the lawyer's office on

Wednesday afternoon to finally sign the damn divorce papers. I want this done, and I'll go in my pyjamas if I have to.

"Yes, I'm still here." She stood up and opened the cupboard door where Joy's key hung on a labelled hook.

"Then get over here with the key!" he barked.

Maggie stared at the dead phone in her hand. It would be at least an hour before Ron got home. She had to call him. "Something's wrong at Joy's. Kurt just phoned and asked me to bring the key."

"Tell him to call the police."

"I haven't heard from her since Tuesday. I need... I can't sit here and wait."

"Maggie, the roads are wicked tonight."

"I'll be careful. I'll call you when I get there."

In the run to the garage, Maggie felt the sting of freezing fog on her face. She gripped the wheel and cursed the black ice streets.

Going to sleep it off. Call me if you need chicken soup. *I'll be fine. No worries. I have the migraine meds. I just got my insulin refilled, and I have a glass of orange juice beside the bed.*

Kurt was standing on the dark front step. Maggie handed the key to him, pinched between her fingers like an insect.

When he gave the key back to her after opening the door, it felt heavier.

"Joy!" Kurt's voice ripped into the silent house. "Joy!"

Straight up the stairs, and Maggie followed.

"Joy!" He opened the bedroom door, flicked the light on, and then off again with just enough time for Maggie to see her friend sprawled on the floor. Kurt turned and stretched out his arms to block her.

She'd seen the tangled sheet; Joy's outstretched arm, reaching. Maggie tried to close her throat to the smell. She needed to go in. There should be a pillow under Joy's head, the quilt from the bed covering her. She tried to push past, but Kurt pulled the door shut.

The howl came from so deep inside her, Maggie felt her guts twist. Kurt put his hand on her shoulder, but she would not let herself feel the warmth of it; she shrugged it away. She would take no comfort from this man. "Phone 911!" she screamed at him.

"Let's go downstairs." He put his hands on her shoulders and steered her to the stairwell. In this nightmare, his palms pressing on her back, she descended the stairs. Breathe. Down. Breathe. Down, hands clutching the banisters.

Maggie wanted him to turn away, face the wall, when he made the phone call, but instead, he stared straight at her. Finally, he put the phone in his pocket and went into the kitchen. He came back to her with a glass of water in his hand. She took three steps backward. Shook her head. Her trembling hand would spill the water before it reached her lips.

Flashing lights outside. Police and ambulance. Kurt, in the lead, everyone following him up the stairs. In spite of what she'd seen and what she knew, Maggie wanted to shout at them to hurry.

A policewoman came back down to the living room and sat beside Maggie.

"This must be a terrible shock," she said. "What is your relationship to the Hartmans, ma'am?"

"My name is Maggie," she croaked. "Joy is my friend."

Heavy footsteps on the stairs. Kurt and the second police officer.

"You came with Mr. Hartman, or on your own?" the woman asked.

"I phoned Maggie and told her to come because she had a key." Kurt taking charge.

A paramedic called from the top of the stairs. "The M.E.'s on her way."

"The medical examiner," the policewoman whispered to Maggie.

"Right away, I knew we were too late," Kurt said. "I knew

from her ankles. The blood pools in the ankles, right? And the smell."

Maggie felt an icicle fall in the back of her skull, straight down her spine. In the split second in the open doorway, he'd seen Joy's ankles?

Kurt pulled out his phone and walked across the room. Calling the other woman. His voice so soft. Calm. Why was he not in shock? Divorce or not, he'd been married to Joy for twenty years. Twenty years.

Through her horror at seeing Joy on the floor, through the mist that had been gathering in Maggie's mind, she walked back to the moments after she handed Kurt the key. Why straight to the bedroom instead of the family room, the main floor?

Maggie's phone was vibrating. Ron. She left that room full of strangers, went into the bathroom, and closed the door.

"Son of a bitch. I'm coming now."

"No," she said, "There are too many people already. I'll be home soon."

In the living room, a woman in a raincoat was taking off her boots at the door. Maggie looked down at her own stockinged feet. She and this new woman were the only ones who'd taken off their wet shoes in Joy's house.

The woman picked up her bag, hoisted it to her shoulder. Kurt led the way up the stairs again.

The young officer came to stand beside her. "This will be over soon. There's nothing you can do. Can we drive you home?" So kind, but Maggie wanted to shout that she could not leave, not while her friend was lying on the bedroom floor.

"Don't I need to sign something? Give a statement?"

"From the information we already have from Mr. Hartman, this is pretty straightforward."

"What did he tell you? Did he tell you Joy was sick with a migraine?" Did he even know that?

"Maggie, there is nothing more you can do." So much kindness in the woman's voice.

Obstinate, Maggie sat down. "I'll wait. I want to know what happened."

"It's not likely the M.E. can say much tonight."

"I'm going to wait." She closed her eyes and willed an image of Joy's smiling face to replace the picture drawn on the bedroom floor.

She felt the air move. Kurt and the doctor coming down the stairs.

"I'm Dr. Fleming," she said. "And you are...?"

"Maggie Whitton." There. Now someone knew her whole name. In case they needed to ask questions. She would tell this doctor about the migraine. "Joy's friend," she whispered.

"Maggie had the house key," Kurt said for the third time. Didn't anyone wonder why Kurt didn't break a window or kick in a door to get to Joy? Even an ex-husband would break a window.

The doctor extended her hand. "They're going to be bringing your friend down any minute. Come wait in the kitchen."

In the kitchen, they were out of view of the stairs and the front door. Surely this woman knew what she was talking about. And yet Maggie wanted to run back and watch these strangers take Joy from her house. There should be a witness to this leaving. Someone who knew Joy.

Kurt opened the cupboard and pulled out prescription bottles. The doctor had two vials in her hand. *I have the pills and I have insulin. Right beside me.*

"We'll check with the pharmacy," the examiner said, "to make sure there weren't any current prescriptions other than the migraine medication and the insulin."

"She tended to over-medicate," Kurt said. "Sometimes she'd forget what she'd taken."

The doctor's eyebrows went up.

What the hell?

He pursed his lips. "There was a problem with alcohol as well. You may not have been aware of this, Maggie."

"There. Was. Not. Joy is diabetic, and she does not drink."

The doctor swung around to face Maggie. "How long have you known Mrs. Hartman?"

"Since we were schoolkids. A lot longer than he has." Maggie thrust her chin in Kurt's direction and then looked away. "Joy told me on Tuesday that she had a migraine. Who dies of a headache?"

There was a commotion on the stairs. "Okay." A calm male voice from the living room. "Straight on."

Then louder, "We're out now, doc."

Dr. Fleming scooped the medications into her bag. "We'll know more in a few days." She looked from Kurt to Maggie. "When was the last time anyone heard from Mrs. Hartman?"

"Tuesday morning," Maggie said, although she didn't know for sure. Maybe someone else had spoken with Joy. There were people she needed to call when she got home.

No answer from Kurt. He had turned away, staring into the darkness beyond the kitchen window.

"You must have seen her after that, Kurt. She was meeting you on Wednesday," Maggie said. *In my pyjamas if I have to.*

"She didn't show up."

"You didn't wonder why? Did you try to find her on Wednesday?"

He swung round with his fists clenched at his sides. "Where the hell have you been since Tuesday, Maggie?"

They stared at each other.

The doctor cleared her throat. Kurt's shoulders sagged, and he turned away again. "What does any of it matter now? What is, is."

Maggie knew how much Joy hated those words. *He came in the door and told me he didn't love me anymore. He found someone else. What is, is. Who says that?*

There were only three of them in the house now. And none of them mattered. Without Joy, this house was empty.

It was ten o'clock. Two hours ago, Maggie had been crushing

eggs to make muffins for her friend. "I'm going home now," she said.

WHEN MAGGIE GOT HOME, Ron was waiting at the window. He opened the door, led her to the sofa, wrapped her in a blanket, came back with Scotch, and said, "Drink." One gulp, she coughed and sputtered, then another greedy gulp, and it was down. "Tell me," he said. "Tell me everything."

When she'd done talking and wept herself dry, she closed her eyes, so grateful that he hadn't stopped her, not once. Not once had he argued, told her to be reasonable. She opened her eyes again.

Ron exhaled. "You don't think he killed her, do you?"

Maggie knew from all the times Joy had cried that Kurt was a liar. Even when he didn't need to, he'd made up stories about where he'd been, and with whom.

She shook and shook and shook her head. "No. No." No, she would not let this question burrow its way into her mind.

"Then what?"

"I don't know. But I do know he still has his bloody key." She felt a rush of blood to her head. "He went into the house, found her, but didn't want to take responsibility? He wants to lay the blame on me."

She made phone calls to one friend, another friend, then one more. They would phone another who would phone another. In a few hours, all of Joy's friends would know that Joy was dead.

It was past one o'clock when Maggie looked around the kitchen again; the muffin mess was still on the table.

"Leave it," Ron said.

Maggie took the key out of her pocket and hung it on the inside of the cupboard door. Under the label that said JOY.

A PRACTICAL WOMAN

THE OLD CAT hunkers on the counter next to the aquarium, more interested in the bloated goldfish now than when it was alive. Moira scoops out the fish, walks toward the kitchen garbage, and shakes her head. She leaves the dripping net on the drain board and picks up the phone. The cat noses the fish through the mesh but doesn't sustain his curiosity or his appetite long enough to persist.

"Time to get down, Steps." Moira hooks an arm under his belly and lowers him to the floor, taking care to let him down gently. She winces every time he jumps off a chair, feeling the jolt in her own arthritic knee.

She turns her attention to the phone. On the fourth ring, youngest son answers.

"Nugget died," she says.

"What?"

"Don't say 'what' to your mother." She's been telling her kids this since they started to talk.

He laughs. "Yeah, okay. Pardon, Mom?"

"Your goldfish died. Nugget. Do you want the tank, or should I put it out with the trash? And how did we dispose of all the other fishy corpses?"

"I guess we flushed them. Nugget isn't mine. Mine's the catfish. The guy who lives under the bridge."

The catfish? Moira peers through the algae-coated wall of the tank. Equally scummed with green, there is a little ceramic bridge resting on a bed of gravel, and under the bridge, a long black shadow lurks.

"Mom? Are you there?"

"We have never flushed a pet. What should I do with the catfish? I'm leaving next week."

"I still vote toilet. He hasn't moved in years. When do you think you'll be back?"

No matter how often Moira tells the kids she's leaving for good, they don't believe her. "But this is home," they say. Home to them, but she's never felt settled out here. Even though she was the one who wanted to pack up three babies and move to Alberta all those years ago. Better jobs, better life for the kids, she'd coaxed her dubious husband. She was right about everything except him. But now that the kids are gone, she has no reason for living here.

"Hey, Mom! Are you still there? What about the rest of the zoo?" He sounds curious but not the least bit concerned.

"I'm working on that. Talk to you later."

She's already given away the garden tools, so she chips at the soil near the back gate with a rusty serving spoon. Probably a good idea to warn the landlord about the pet cemetery in case the new tenant is a gardener. One large dog buried deep and safe, two cats, rabbits without number, gerbils, hamsters. She imagines the back lane cordoned off, the entire yard turfed over, men in coveralls sifting, dropping bone fragments into Ziploc baggies.

She's wrapped the fish in an envelope of waxed paper. She lays it in the shallow bowl of earth and strategically spreads lumps of dirt. Dissatisfied with the coverage, she decides to finish the job with a layer of cat litter.

The box is overdue for a cleaning. She can smell it as soon as she walks down the basement stairs. Steps, now asleep on a piece of old carpet beside the furnace, opens one eye when he hears her scraping in his box.

"Go back to sleep," she says. "I'll worry about you later."

"I THOUGHT I'd better let you know that I'm giving Sookie to the woman at the bakery."

The little dog is asleep on her blanket, but opens black marble eyes when she hears her name announced to the daughter's answering machine.

"What?" There's a click, and the familiar voice interrupts her recording. So like her own voice, it always takes Moira by surprise. "Mom? What are you talking about?"

"So, you are there after all?"

"Of course, I'm here. Is this some kind of sick joke, saying you're giving my dog away just to get my attention?"

Moira holds the phone away from her ear, and Sookie bounds off the couch, skittering across the bare hardwood. "I'm leaving for Moncton at the end of the week. It'll be too hard to find a place that takes pets, and I can't drive across the country with this menagerie anyway." She picks up the dog with her free hand, hoping the snuffly whimpers will carry all the way to Toronto. "That woman who's been at the bakery for years, you know the one with the birthmark? Her Shih Tzu died this winter, and she was heartbroken."

"You're giving my dog to a stranger?"

"You're welcome to fly out and get her," she says. Doesn't mention that she'll be stopping overnight in Toronto. She's already decided that if there are too many tears, she'll bring the dog. She hasn't really spoken to the bakery woman yet.

"You know I can't do that. I'd have to move. Do you know

how hard that is in this city? You expect me to find another apartment because you're tired of looking after Sookie?"

"Just plain tired. Let me know by tomorrow night if you change your mind. Do you remember who the goldfish belongs to?"

"The what?"

"The goldfish. Nugget."

"I didn't know we had fish. The turtles were mine. I don't have room for a fish tank. Have to run, Mom. Kiss Sookie goodbye for me."

Moira hangs up and stares into the dog's pug face. Just like that. If she'd known it would be easy, she would have shed this one three years ago when the daughter moved out. Sookie has never liked Moira, and the feeling is mutual. *Goodbye, snooty little dog.*

NEXT, a call to the animal shelter to ask if they take birds.

"What kind of bird, Ma'am?"

"Lovebird."

"Pair?'"

"No. Single." She doesn't report that Tony the lovebird has had three mates, all of them mysteriously dead within a month. That the pet store has repeatedly said Tony would never survive as a widower, and yet here he is, fifteen years later.

"Sometimes," the cautious voice says, "we can place them. Especially if it's a young bird, friendly. Is he hand-trained? Can he talk?"

Already, this is a lost cause. Talk? No. He shrieks. When the house is quiet, he screeches until she turns on the television or the radio or opens the cage and lets him cruise. Tony hates children and is selective even with adults. A good judge of character, the kids said when the bird tried to take a chunk out of the chin of one of the few men Moira dated in the fifteen years after their dad split.

Her children had pooled their money for the first Mother's Day without their dad. Too young to appreciate the irony of giving their single mother a pair of lovebirds, they hatched their plan in the conservatory at the zoo. Really, Moira hadn't even noticed what she was looking at until they pointed. "Do you like those birds?" they wanted to know.

She shrugged. "Sure. They're cute."

This was the way every animal except Steps came into their lives. "Do you like rabbits, Mom?"

"Sure. They're cute." Then a quick scurry to the back step, and the child would be back with a rescued bunny in his arms.

It's years since Moira's been to the zoo. She phones her eldest son, remembering that he took the kids to see the baby giraffe the last time they were here visiting.

"I don't suppose you'd want Tony," she says.

"As in Tony the psycho lovebird? Not likely. I'd prefer your grandkids to grow up with all their fingers."

"Do they still have birds in the conservatory at the zoo?"

"I don't know," he says. "We spent all our time at the snack bar."

STEPS WEAVES a wobbly path to Moira's chair when she sits down to watch the news. She scoops the cat onto her lap and runs her hand over his greasy coat.

"He's losing interest in grooming himself," the vet said last year. And that reminds her that she forgot to crush the thyroid medication into the cat food this morning. Easing the warm burden from her knees, she goes into the kitchen for a bowl, opens the freezer for the ice cream, and stirs the tiny tablet into a melting puddle.

"Treat time, Steps. I don't have many goodies left for you."

When Steps has finished licking the bowl, Moira reaches down and then cradles the cat in her arms. Sookie springs off her own chair on the other side of the room and gambols over to claim a share of the attention.

In the kitchen, Tony has begun to squawk. Time to throw the cover on his cage. The air pump in the aquarium burbles away.

"I'll get rid of the rest of the gang tomorrow," Moira whispers to the cat, "and we'll have a bit of peace."

SHE SCRUBS THE FISH TANK, washes the gravel, and sets the whole kit out in the back lane beside the garbage can. "FREE," says the note she tapes to the side. "HELP YOURSELF." This has worked for countless items over the years. After Moira's husband hopped a bus one morning instead of going to work, and she found out he'd gone "home," back east to his old job, his old life, she'd hung his suits on the rails of the fence and let the kids set up a table and sell his books and records. Recycling. She's good at shedding possessions responsibly. A practical woman.

Moira gets into the car with the catfish in his margarine container of smelly water. The creek is a short drive away.

She crouches in the muddy weeds and tips the fish to freedom. When he sinks in the shallows and winds himself into the shadow of a rock, she turns and walks away, taking the plastic tub home to the recycling bin.

THE BAKERY WOMAN is waiting in front of Moira's house when she drives up. The woman's smile slices through the deep wine stain on her cheek. "I know I'm early, but I couldn't wait," she says and then blinks and looks away. "I guess I was afraid you might change your mind."

Sookie skitters to the door to meet them, and when the woman crouches, the little dog scrambles into her arms as though she's been waiting all her life for this saviour.

The tattered blue blanket, the bag of toys, a case of dog food, and the stainless steel bowls are all stashed in the woman's little car. When she's driven away, the house seems cold and very still.

Moira turns on the radio and sets the kettle to make tea. Steps wanders into the kitchen. From the remnants of the pantry now packed in two boxes on the counter, Moira scrounges sardines. The cat waits patiently, leaning against Moira's ankle while she unfurls the top of the can and lays one oily fish on a saucer. She'll save the rest to have on toast. "Fresh fish back home, Kitty," she says. "Lobster, the first night in." The cat coughs and retches up the half-chewed sardine. Moira phones the vet and makes an appointment two days away.

ELDEST SON CALLS HOME that night, offering to come out and help her pack. "Have you booked a van, Mom?"

Moira reaches across the bedroom floor to drag the phone closer. Because she'd been asleep for more than an hour when the phone rang, it takes her a minute to collect her thoughts. The room is empty except for the mattress and the suitcases and boxes along the wall.

"No van," she tells him. "I'm travelling light. I won't need any help. But I'll stop for a quick visit." She's already planned an overnight stay in Regina. Always a pleasure to share her grandsons' room so they can giggle together in the bottom bunk.

"I'm nervous for you, Mom, but glad too. We'll come out for Christmas this year."

He's been making regular trips to the East Coast for years, this boy, the only one of the three who's forgiven their dad for bailing and visits with him as well as with aunts and uncles and cousins on both sides.

"Hey, it sounds like you're sweeping the nest clean. What are you doing about Steps?" he asks.

Moira looks to the end of the bed, where the old cat is nested in the folds of her velour housecoat. Steps belongs to all of the kids, the third cat they acquired after two short-lived kittens. Their dad went out early the morning after they'd chipped a hole in the half-frozen November garden to bury cat number two. When he came back, the older kids were at the table, the youngest in his high chair, all staring glumly into bowls of Cheerios. He pulled a bedraggled kitten from his pocket. "Look what I found on the back steps," he said.

"Mom? Are you there? Do you want to leave Steps with us?"

She shakes her head. Her daughter-in-law has asthma. The cat looks up with one eye, the other caked with pus. Moira needs to press a warm cloth to it every morning. "No," she says, "I couldn't do that."

Youngest son phones ten minutes later when she's in the kitchen eating toast and sardines. She's mashed the fish for Steps this time and lifted him to the counter where he crouches in front of her, scarfing up the snack, one eye on the dish and the crusted one on her, unable to believe this indulgence.

"Hi, Mom. Sorry to call so late. I always forget about the hour's difference."

He offers to fly home on the weekend. To help her get away. They're such fine boys, Moira thinks, staring into the dark beyond the kitchen window, the smell of fish oiling the back of her throat.

"Honestly, I don't need any help," she tells him. She wishes he were also on her route, but Vancouver is in the opposite direction. "Fly out at Christmas instead. I'm hoping all of you will come." She's sure they will. Their older brother will convince them and probably convince them to visit their dad as well. If they haven't already. Moira never asks.

"What are you going to do out there, Mom? You're way too

young to retire." And too poor, but she doesn't remind him of this.

"Nurses are in short supply everywhere. I've already lined up some interviews."

The phone doesn't have a chance to cool before it shrills again. She's sure it's her daughter, but instead, another familiar voice hits her like a big dog to the back of her knees. She clutches the counter.

"Hello? Moira? Are you still there?"

"Yeah." She hoists herself onto the cupboard, one foot braced against the sink.

"I hear you're coming back."

His voice hasn't changed. In fact, it's deeper and more mellow than it was in the last phone call when she told him she never wanted to hear from him again. "Finally quit smoking, eh?"

He laughs. "How can you tell? You're too far away to smell my clothes."

"Your voice," she says. "I figured you'd sound like your dad by now."

"Nah, after the heart attack, I decided I didn't have any choice. You knew I had heart trouble a few years back?"

So she'd heard, from their eldest. At the time, she wished he'd die. Hearing his voice again, she's probably glad he didn't. "No," she lies. "And I guess I don't need to hear about it now. What do you want?"

"Lord God Almighty, you haven't changed a bit. I wanted to tell you I'm glad you're coming back. I know you hate it out there even though you're too stubborn to admit it."

"Look, I have a lot to do here. Packing and getting rid of all these damn pets."

"Yeah, I guess you do. Why don't you call me when you get in?"

"Why would I want to do that?"

Steps has wandered into the kitchen looking dazed and stares up at her as though he'd give anything to make the leap to the counter. But he can't. Instead, he yowls.

"What the hell is that?"

"The cat. One of the many responsibilities you walked out on."

"The same old cat? What was his name again? Steps, right? Still alive after all these years?"

"Barely," she says. She slides off the counter and crouches beside Steps. He stops howling and winds himself around her leg, his purring rough and mucousy.

"Aw, you're not planning on doing away with Steps before you leave? Christ, if he's lived this long, he'll make it another three thousand miles. Bring him along. I'll take him."

She feels such a rush of rage, she growls into the phone. "How dare you offer to help now. You dumped me when I needed you most!"

She hangs up the phone and sits a long while, crying, with the trusting weight of the cat leaning warm against her shin.

Finally, she's aware of Tony keening. Never has she heard him mimic so well. She opens the cage door and lets him perch on her shoulder, where he bobs his head, regurgitating seed, trying to deposit it in her ear. He's never needed another Cleo. She's been enough for this feathery little Anthony.

MOIRA'S IS one of the first cars into the zoo parking lot. Only a few moms pushing strollers full of early-rising babies and toddlers make their way to the entrance. The landscape has changed since she was last here. There's a new entrance, and the skeleton of massive new construction rises over the old buildings. But still, she can see the conservatory flanked by flower beds mulched and ready for snow.

Tony is on the passenger seat in a hamster cage salvaged from the last of the boxes she piled on the front step this morning for the Goodwill pick-up. After screeching all the way, when the car stops, Tony is suddenly silent and huddles into the corner of the cage, trembling.

Moira lifts him out and holds his little body in front of her nose. He tilts his head to stare at her. Such an exotic treasure with his peach-coloured face, the fan of turquoise tail against the moss green of his body. He feels like velvet when she brings him to her cheek.

Fortunately, he's always loved to hide in pockets.

By the time she walks to the conservatory, pushes through the protective double entry that keeps the birds in and the weather out, he's twitching and starting to squawk. There are two young people in uniforms leaning against the counter at the snack bar, and one little family on the path. Tony's calls blend with the chitter of rainbow birds flitting through the lush greenery.

Moira faces the waterfall in the farthest corner from the snack bar and waits until a little boy who's trying desperately to wet his chubby hand has gone back to his mother.

She lifts Tony out of her pocket, his heart pounding against her palm, and hides him against the front of her jacket. When she relaxes her fingers, he stays cupped in her hand. Even when she gently slides her hand away, he clings to her lapel. But then, a small orange bird lights in the hibiscus in front of her, and in a flash of green, Tony is gone, blending perfectly into the tropical forest. Knowing that it's only a matter of time before he returns to her shoulder, she leaves quickly and doesn't look back.

WHILE MOIRA PACKS the car and sweeps the house clean, Steps sits in the middle of the kitchen looking confused. His head swivels side to side, following her progress. Finally, she makes one last circuit of the empty rooms and picks up the cat. She wishes she had a carrier today. For years, they put Steps in a pillowcase for trips to the vet. They discovered by accident that he stayed oddly quiet if he was bundled blind and held tightly. The last time, he was too sick to care, and she laid him in the front seat.

The cat stiffens when Moira opens the car door and almost springs from her arms before she can slide inside. When the door is closed, she lets go, and he leaps from her arms to the floor in the back and crouches there howling.

Fortunately, it's a short drive to the animal clinic, but it takes Moira five minutes to coax Steps out from under the seat. The waiting room is packed. One look at Moira's face, a glance at the appointment schedule, and the receptionist takes her through to an empty examining room. By the time the vet comes in, the cat is calmed in her arms, but clawing tight to the front of her sweater.

"Well, if it isn't my old friend, Steps."

She's pleased they've drawn the most senior of the doctors today, a soft-hearted Scotsman who miraculously pulled Steps through distemper a week after he was "found" on the back steps.

She swallows hard. "I'm moving," she says, "and there's no one to take him."

The vet cups a gentle hand over the cat's ears, crouches down to look in his eyes. "Actually," he says quietly, "he doesn't look too bad at all. But frail, eh? And comes a time . . ."

Steps looks from one to the other of them and begins to purr.

There's a tap on the door. A phone call for the doctor. He takes Moira's elbow and steers her gently to a chair. "You just sit a minute. I won't be long."

He told her once long ago in his soft Scottish brogue that cats are his favourite animals. She nodded. Hers too.

Moira thinks about the catfish in the clear stream, Tony perched high on a bougainvillea vine, Sookie nibbling pastry treats, red bows in her freshly clipped hair. And Nugget.

She opens the door and carries Steps out to the car without waiting for the vet. He'll understand.

The pillowcase is easy to find in the suitcase of linen in the trunk. Steps goes limp when she eases him into the cloth bag and puts him on the passenger seat. Moira keeps one hand on the pillowcase while she pulls into traffic. She's sure that by the time they leave the city, Steps will find his way out. It's a long journey, and he'll be good company.

TRESPASSES

SYLVIA SLAMS the window so hard the glass ripples. Aftershock reverberates through her shoulders, but her neighbour doesn't look up. Deafened by his weed whacker, he's sculpting a fussy property line. Every *tziiiitt* means Walter has felled another clump of lily-of-the-valley. Sylvia grips the edge of the desk. Without that mooring, she'd sail out the door, rip the weed eater out of his hands, and use it to carve her initials in the perfect steel helmet of his hair.

Finally, there's blessed silence. Closing her eyes, she releases the pen, lets go of the swirl of platitudes in her head, and welcomes the thick absence of sound and thought.

She'd make a pot of tea and take her cup into the sunshine, but years of living next door to Walter and Doris have etched their garden routine on her brain. Surely as thunder follows lightning, the Toro will charge across the lawn now that the edging is done.

She dares a peek, sliding the streaky pane of glass along a gritty track. Really, she needs to spring clean—dust blinds, polish windows, slap stain on the fence—but each time she approaches the jobs she and Steve did together for thirty-nine years, her ears strain to hear his tuneless humming. The small of her back aches for his hand when she lifts the bucket of soapy water he would have carried.

The screen is redolent with dust. Next door, the windows gleam, and Sylvia imagines Doris with spray bottle and cloth in hand.

Tomorrow. Today, the thank-you notes are three months overdue.

*For your kindness and support while Steven was ill . . .*The same numb thank-you over and over, but for family members, extra assurance that life goes on. *You were right when you said I would feel as though there's a stone in my chest. I think the back of my throat has turned to granite. But the weather's fine here now. Tomorrow, I'll tackle the perennial beds.*

A line through her sister-in-law's name on the list, one more envelope sealed and stamped, and then the lawnmower fades to the back.

While the kettle boils, Sylvia leans on the counter and eats cottage cheese from the plastic tub. Why dirty one plate, pull one chair askew from the table? She pours directly into a cup, jerking the string on the teabag until the water is amber and fragrant with bergamot.

Steaming tea in hand, she soaks up sun on the front step, face tilted to the warmth, bare feet curled against the cold cement. When the cup is empty, she wanders onto the grass, stopping short of the property line. Her toes fit neatly into the lush green scallops where Walt's fertilizer has leached into her lawn.

"Sylvia!" Tall and gaunt in his beltless grey coveralls, Walt curls over her like a plume of smoke. "We need to talk about the trailer."

Sylvia glances over her shoulder at the unfenced strip of property between their houses. The utility trailer that Walt and Steve went halves on years ago sits on a patch of gravel straddling the two yards. It hasn't been used since the last time Steve hauled manure. As always, Walt staged a production worthy of an Oscar, hosing and muttering, even though Steve left the trailer as clean as he'd found it. Sylvia had fumed. "If you don't go over there and give him a piece of your mind, I will."

Steve's blue eyes peered over his newspaper. "Syl, please. That's like pouring kerosene on fire. Just ignore him. We've been neighbours all these years and we'll be neighbours for many more."

Sylvia draws a deep breath, trying to invoke the spring fragrance of horse manure. A light broadcasting over the rose beds inspired Steve's crimson *Europeana* to produce blooms as big as soup bowls.

When he stops picking at spruce galls on the lowest branches of her tree, Walt squints into the tower of green. "Must be dark as a tomb in there with this thing blocking your bedroom window." When she doesn't answer, lost still in memories of roses, he advances a step. "I warned Steve twenty years ago he was planting too near the house."

"What do you want?" She slides between Walter and the tree, forcing him back onto his own property, so close she can smell coffee on his breath. He's on his break, the quiet just an interlude. "About the trailer? What do you want to know?"

"Can I sell it? I'll clean up that corner with some sod."

Sylvia's head shakes as soon as she hears "sell." Every time the kids come over, someone drags out "sell."

"No." She rattles calendar leaves in her mind. This must be May. Time for a trip to the mushroom farm. "The garden needs a load of manure."

Sylvia knows that a year ago, before Steve died, before everyone began handling her with velvet gloves, Walt would have snorted and told her what her garden needed was a good dose of Roundup.

"Aw, Syl," he rolls the words around his mouth. "Just hire someone to look after the yard."

Like hell she will. She can't bear the thought of trespassers in the garden, even though she promised Steve she'd stay away from the power tools.

"Please be sensible when I'm gone," he'd said, his hands on her shoulders. His touch, by then, had all the weight of a shadow. "I keep imagining you cutting grass in your bare feet."

She promised to leave the power mower in the garage and use the push mower. She loves the clackety-clack and the spray of green confetti on her toes. She also promised she'd look after his roses.

"I'm taking the trailer out next weekend. My half stays, Walt. Do what you want with yours." But does she remember how they hooked up the trailer? Does she have the strength to do it alone?

Sylvia turns so quickly she staggers in a whirl of vertigo. Shrugging away the steadying arm Walt offers, she plods back to the house. Inside, she drags out the phone book and calls the mushroom farm. She's just in time. Today, tomorrow, and Sunday, there's an "all you can load" special at the manure pile.

Next, she phones David. "Could you stop by on your way home from work tomorrow and help me hitch up the trailer? I'm going to the mushroom farm."

"Mom!" There's gentle exasperation in his voice. "Why?"

"Because it's time." She leans on the kitchen counter, staring out at the crabapple, all a-flounce with white.

"Why don't you ask Walter to share a load? I'm sure he'd pick it up."

"Walter doesn't use manure in his garden. He's been whining about the stink from ours for years."

"Try him anyway. I have to work tomorrow. Last time I was over, he caught me on the way to the car and said he wanted to help. He said he offered to fertilize the lawn, and you told him to get lost."

"I never. I told him if I need his help, I know where to find him." Through the kitchen window, she can see Walt sweeping cobwebs off the eaves of his garage.

A robin lands on a branch of the crabapple, a bit of red string dangling from its beak, and dives into the centre of the tree. "Oh, David! The robin's back." The sight of that cheerful bird sends tears tracking the grooves from Sylvia's cheeks to her mouth.

"Let Walter help, Mom. He's a good neighbour."

"Of course he is, but he's irritating, and he's . . ." She tastes salt at the corner of her lips and dabs at her eyes with a tea towel. "Never mind, David. I'll think of something."

Her hand is too shaky to finish the cards, and she's run out of words. Sylvia tucks her hair under Steve's sweat-stained baseball cap and digs a pair of gumboots out of the closet. She clomps out to the trailer and contemplates the hitch, running her palm over ridges of rust, trying to remember how Steve's hands married metal to metal.

The car is backed onto the gravel, the metal tongue on the trailer licking the hitch, when Walt looms up out of a clump of juniper. "Sylvia, what the hell are you doing?"

"Good God! Don't sneak around like that." One hand on her throat, she steadies herself on the trailer with the other. "Is it your hearing or your memory that's failing you? I told you I'm going for manure."

Three long strides bring him so close she's trapped against the trailer. Then he gets a cagey look, a little twitching around the lips, and tightening of eyes. "The hitch is broken. See?" He steps forward and rattles a dangling link of chain. "Safety's gone."

Sylvia leans in and hauls down on the latch with both hands, and the hitch locks over the ball. Two side steps, a dash to the car door, key in the ignition, and she's spinning gravel. "It'll be fine," she shouts through the open window.

For the first ten minutes of the drive, she sucks on the four broken nails on her left hand. The drive is longer than she remembers, but the wait at the manure pile is short. This late in the day, the serious gardeners have come and gone. Sylvia's the last in line, and after the backhoe dumps a pungent load into her trailer, she rolls away, and the iron gate clangs shut behind her.

All the way home, she keeps one eye through the rearview mirror on the swaying deck of the trailer. When she cranks the window closed to shut out the jangle of the broken chain, the car smells faintly of Players, even though it's three years since Steve quit smoking. "Yeah, yeah," she mutters, "I know. Be sensible. I'm trying, sweetheart. Honest, I am."

No sign of Walt when she maneuvers the trailer onto the front lawn, nor through the long hour of flinging manure. Eyes stinging, throat raw from the stench, Sylvia scrapes the last lumps from the trailer, then jumps down and, with the back of the shovel, pounds a flat face onto the pile where it rides the edge of Walter's lawn.

As though he's been waiting the four hours since she left, Walt is framed in his open garage door with the hose when she drives around back. His lips are pressed in a purple line. "Leave it in the alley!" he barks. "Or I'll wash the shit onto your side of the yard."

Sylvia pulls in close to the fence. The car can stay out until tomorrow, and the mountain of manure can grace the front lawn until David has time to help her spread it. For all she cares, Walt can set fire to the trailer. Still, she gives him a jaunty salute before she sprints to the back door. Then she kicks off the stinking boots, sinks onto the steps in the back entry, and rests her head against the wall until she has the strength to run a hot bath.

After a long soak in the tub and an hour dozing in front of the television, she falls into bed and instantly into sleep. But at one-thirty, Sylvia's eyes fly open.

All those years of nudging Steve, growling at him to roll over, turn off the buzz-saw, and now that she has silence, she suffers more than ever from sleeplessness. Tiny, frantic insects scratch and crawl under her skin. Red-eyed mice race in the wire cages of her mind. She tosses and turns, and finally pads down the hall in her nightgown.

A full moon hangs in the kitchen window. The refrigerator light is all she needs to pour a cup of milk, warm it in the microwave, and drag a chair into the puddle of moonbeams in the middle of the floor. When the cup is rinsed and set on the drainboard to dry, Sylvia leans into the window, face pressed to the screen. But she wants to feel the night like velvet on her cheek, and moves impulsively to the back door.

Barefoot on the cool grass, she can see a faint light in the kitchen window next door. Like Sylvia just minutes before, Doris stands in front of the refrigerator. When she turns, holding the milk carton, Sylvia's hand lifts in an involuntary wave, but she's relieved that Doris doesn't respond. In the turning, Sylvia sees that Doris is naked in her kitchen.

Before Sylvia can tactfully turn her attention to the moon, Walt slides pale and tall into the tableau. Two of them, naked in the night, padding together down the hall to share a glass of milk.

Sylvia closes her eyes, but can still see how Doris's shoulders will lift when she feels Walt behind her, how she will lean ever so slightly forward to fit his body to the curves of her own. How the man will cup his wife's breasts with warm, sure hands, encircle her. How he will reach into the back of the cupboard for the bottle of rye, add a generous splash to the warm milk, and hold the cup for her to sip. "Night cap," he'll say, his hand sliding from her cheek down the slope of her neck, her back, and then coming to rest on a pillowy buttock. And then he'll pull her close.

In the silent moonlit movie Sylvia watches on the dark screen of her eyelids, the wife lifts her face for the familiar taste of her husband's lips, then takes his hand and leads him back to bed.

When Sylvia opens her eyes, Doris and Walt's kitchen window is dark. Thankfully, a cloud has scudded across the moon. Doris would be mortified if she knew her neighbour was spying from under the ceiling of crabapple blossom. And what about Walt?

"The old fool," Sylvia whispers. But that isn't it. As she tried to tell David, the problem with Walt is that he's . . . alive.

And so is Sylvia. She knows this because she feels blades of grass sharp between her toes, catches a whiff of manure on the wind, tastes apple scent on the back of her throat, and hears the heavy thud of heartbeat against her breastbone.

ELEPHANTS

MY BROTHER WENT MISSING for five years, except for the rare contact with our mother. After his constant calls to me prior to the silence, I was relieved. But he was my brother, my only brother, so I occasionally tried to connect. The phone numbers Mom supplied were always "no longer in use." She remembered small bits of conversation with Jake that became confusing even as she was passing them along.

Then came a significant update. Jacob was with a new woman whose name Mom couldn't remember. But this one seemed better than any of the others, especially the one he'd married. "I think he's going to be okay, Peter!" Mom told me. "I believe he said he was going to buy a ring!" That there might finally be someone to look after Jacob had lifted the fog and given our mother a moment of clarity.

Jake's women were the least of the things I'd dealt with. For more than twenty years before he dropped out of sight, shady business deals, bad investments, extravagant spending, and his tapping into Mom's small savings had been constant. My wife and I had left Edmonton and moved to Calgary after we were married, but Jake assured me that bank transfers to meet his needs would work just fine.

Weddings and funerals and other reunions of our large extended family were events Jake had loved. He would drive up in a flashy new car, new suit, grin on his face, larger than life. He stole the show. He was our dad's favourite, and no matter how deep the trouble he landed in, he was "just Jake." Boys will be boys. I, on the other hand, was never just a boy. I was the older brother. I'd wondered if, in the ten years I was his only child, Dad ever puffed out his chest and laughed at my "escapades." Except that I was not a child prone to escapades.

After Dad died and wasn't there to bail him out, Jake called *me* when he needed a fix. Cash was almost always the solution. I admit that bossing Jake around had come naturally since we were in short pants, even though he rarely complied. *Sure. I'll do that right now.* And he'd carry on exactly as he had been. Giving me the responsibility of looking out for Mom seemed to suit him perfectly.

SHORTLY AFTER MOM'S excitement about Jake's new woman, he called me. He and Nadine were getting married. They'd found a commissioner to do the deed, and there would be no fuss or celebration. No guests; neither Mom nor my wife, Heather, nor I were invited. "Nadine likes to keep things simple." A total reversal from the ceremony at the cathedral in downtown Edmonton that the first wife insisted on in her knock-off Princess Diana gown.

Heather took the phone and suggested to Jake that he and Nadine come to Calgary for a visit and bring Mom along. "She must be feeling hurt about not having the chance to meet Nadine, and even more about missing her boy's wedding." He said they'd think about it.

I tried to ask him where he'd been hiding, but he brushed me off. He was in Vancouver mostly. He was "in business" with someone he knew I wouldn't like. He'd come back to Edmonton a few months ago when things weren't going so well. He'd met Nadine, and he didn't want me sticking my oar into his business.

After the wedding, Jake went MIA once again. None of our extended family nor any of Jake's buddies had heard from him. No one had ever met Nadine.

It was as though he'd left the planet. I might have been relieved that I could officially resign as my brother's keeper except for Mom's constant fretting and the fact that she was declining rapidly.

Two years after the wedding, Mom died. Her address book had an entire page dedicated to "Jacob." Entry after entry crossed out, except for one. The final addition was for "Jacob and Nadine." He'd given her that much. I was furious when I saw that he was within walking distance of the nursing home where Mom had lived—lonely, confused, and waiting for her boy.

Jake and Nadine's home was a small, well-tended bungalow. Jake came outside when I rang the bell, and we sat on a bench under a weeping willow.

"You do know that she lived ten minutes away from here, right?" I asked after he'd swiped some tears away. He shook his head. "No, I guess you wouldn't have known," I said, "because you ghosted her as well as me."

"I didn't ghost anyone. Nadine and I just want to have our own life."

I opened my mouth to object, but he cut me off. "Mom was pretty old, eh?"

I wanted to shake him.

At the funeral, we finally met Nadine. She bore no resemblance to the previous women we'd known in Jake's life. Heather estimated she was at least five years older than Jake. Smart dresser but nothing flashy; no false eyelashes, sculpted cheeks, or flaming scarlet lips. As soon as the service was over, she disappeared. Had to get back to work, Jake said. "That's the way it is when you have your own business," he told us, a proud smile on his face.

I asked him what kind of business. Accounting, he said. We never saw Nadine again.

I expected that the funeral would be a turning point and that Jake would update me when his phone numbers changed. By that time, I should have known better. Still, on occasional business trips to Edmonton, I drove by Jake and Nadine's home, but there was never a response when I rang the doorbell. By the time I retired, Jake and Nadine had been married for almost ten years. There was no longer a need for trips to Edmonton. I could assume that Jake was settled and happy. He didn't need me.

Then, Heather and I went to a wedding in Edmonton, and I secretly welcomed the excuse to go back to our hometown. *One more time*, I thought. We drove by the house. The place looked abandoned; dark curtains drawn against the front windows, and a field of thistles dancing in the mulch under the weeping willow. No response when I knocked on the door.

"Isn't it likely they might have moved. Retired, the two of them, sold this place, bought a condo, and off travelling?" Heather said.

I shrugged. Considering Jake's pride when he told us Nadine was an accountant, and because she was older than Jake, early "retirement" from whatever he'd been doing wasn't too far-fetched. Still.

On the drive home, I told myself once more that I was letting go for good. *The ball's in your court, brother—if they play tennis on Jupiter.*

Barely a month after that trip, a phone call just before midnight.

"Pete. Nadine's gone!" Jake sounded as though he was being strangled.

"Where are you?"

"At the hospital," he croaked, and then someone else took the phone.

"Your brother's wife was admitted a week ago, and he's been

with her since then." She spoke quietly. "She passed away tonight."

"She died? Of what?"

"You'll have to ask him for the details. Her body's gone down to the morgue, and he's refusing to leave the unit. Security is taking him to Emergency. He told us you'd be picking him up, so you can find him there." She sounded like she'd worked too many shifts.

It had been snowing most of the day. The highway between Calgary and Edmonton was notoriously wicked in any weather event, and I sure as hell wasn't driving it in the dark.

He's your brother. I wanted to hit the mute button on the Mom voice in my mind; Jake had ghosted me, and now she haunted me.

I sighed. My brother's wife was dead, and he was weeping beside a tired nurse.

"Yes, of course," I told the nurse. "I can be there tomorrow. Meanwhile, I'll try to find someone who can pick him up tonight."

"What's going on, Peter?" Heather had gone to bed early while I sat reading. She stood beside my chair, rubbing her eyes.

"Jake. He's been sitting a death watch for a week. Nadine died today, and he needs to go home."

Heather was wide awake now. "You have to go, Peter. I'll make some strong coffee."

I pointed to the window. "Tonight? I don't think so. I'll go in the morning and try to find someone who can pick him up now."

I hauled out an old address book and thumbed through pages of surnames the same as mine. "Ronnie," I said. "Ronnie and Jake punked around together in the old days."

I'd forgotten that it was past midnight. It took my cousin only a few fuzzy minutes to absolve himself. He and his wife hadn't seen Jake in years. Neither, he said, had any of the other cousins, so far as he knew. He was sorry, but he couldn't go. He wouldn't know what to do with Jake.

At 7 a.m., I was out the door. The snow had stopped, and there was one lane cleared; cars and semis in the ditch, and a lot of other fools trying to get through. It took almost five hours to drive those three hundred kilometres.

"I'm here, Pete." A man slumped in a chair just inside the hospital's Emergency doors held out his hand. If he hadn't spoken, I would have passed him by. Jake was unshaven, his hair was greasy and had crept below the neckline of his sweatshirt, and the rumpled sweats he was wearing looked beyond salvaging.

I knelt in front of him. "Come on, Jake. Let's get you home. Do you have a car in the parkade?"

"No. Somebody stole our car."

I didn't ask for details. It was simpler that way.

For the entire drive, Jake held his face in his hands and sobbed. When I parked in front of the house, he refused to budge. The curtains were drawn, and under the weeping willow, weeds were still thriving under a thin blanket of snow. "Okay. I'm not going to carry you. Just give me the key."

I unlocked the door and stepped into darkness as heavy as the stench. When I pulled the curtains open, dust flew out like moths. A hospital bed made the room barely passable. A walker and commode were parked at the end of the bed. No other furniture but a wall-mounted television, a sofa with a nest of rumpled blankets, and curiously, a family of elephants. A mother, about a metre tall, with two teenagers and a baby, seemed to be marching out of the living room at a slight angle that suggested she was on her way to the kitchen. They were of light wood and easy to move. Much later, I wondered why I'd moved them. And where I'd put them.

While I waited for Jake to shuffle his way from the car to the door, Heather called on my cell. "Give him a hug and tell him I'm so sorry he's lost Nadine."

I'd felt ashamed at the hospital that I could not put my arms around the sad man in the chair. Heather wouldn't have hesitated.

Jake went straight to the sofa and sat with a stained pillow clutched to his chest. After tying up a garbage bag reeking of rotten food and kicking it out the back door, I dragged a kitchen chair in front of the sofa. Jake smelled, the house smelled, and I was going to smell by the time I left this place. "Would you please tell me what's been going on?"

Jake waved a shaky hand at the hospital bed. "Nadine's dead!" he moaned.

He needed to sleep, but I wanted some answers before he crashed. Nadine had cancer, and then a stroke "a while back"— about two years ago, when I eventually pieced together the bits. Good thing he wasn't working, because he could look after her when she came home from the hospital. A week ago, she'd had another stroke and fallen, and when he couldn't get her up, he had to call an ambulance.

"It's been just the two of you? No one able to help?" On the snowy highway, I'd been hoping there was someone else who could help prop up this grieving brother. "What about Nadine's family?"

"Dead. Her mom and dad are dead. She has two sisters, but they're gone... somewhere. One's in Australia, I think, and the other one... maybe Ireland." He looked up at me with bloodshot eyes. "Quit asking me questions. What does her family matter? We don't need anybody. We like to be on our own."

"And now, Jake, you truly are on your own. Go into the bedroom and sleep a while."

He ignored me, curled up on the sofa, and closed his eyes.

I opened windows despite the cold. There was no way we were spending the night in this house. Jake could sleep a bit, shower, and we'd be gone.

One quick glance at the bathroom, though, was enough. There was a pile of rank towels on the floor, an unflushed toilet, a waste basket overflowing with tissues crumpled around secretions the origins of which I didn't want to know. I looked back into the living room. Jacob, always the snappy dresser, the one with the quick one-liners that kept everyone laughing, was reduced to a sobbing, stinking man. I stood for a moment, looking at him. Still my brother. I'd have to walk him into the hotel just as he was.

In the bedroom, I threw underwear, socks, jeans, and a sweatshirt into a bag. Then I stretched out on the bed that looked as though it hadn't been slept in since the last time someone changed the linens. In fact, the bedroom was an oasis of cleanliness. The early morning, the drive, and the past few hours had done me in. When I woke up, it was dark beyond the window. This was January, after all, the darkest time of year. It was five o'clock.

Jake was still asleep. I leaned over him. "Come on, Jake. We're getting out of here for the night."

"I don't want to go."

"We'll come back in the morning," I pulled him up by his arms, surprised at the lack of resistance.

At the hotel, I left Jake in his room to shower and went out to get a bottle of Crown Royal—my brother's poison of preference, as I remembered it—and some takeout.

An hour later, we had a drink and burgers. He wolfed down the food as though he hadn't eaten in a week. Which was entirely possible, but his thirst for the booze was even more dramatic. I left Jake sprawled out and snoring. In my own room, so tired I didn't dare go anywhere near the bed, I sat on a chair at the window and phoned Heather.

"I wonder if your mom knew that Nadine had cancer? Did she go into remission? Why didn't Jake call us when she had the stroke? Can you imagine poor Jake looking after her all this time? How will he get through the grief without help?" Why? How? Who? I ended the conversation after the third time she invoked "poor Nadine!"

I was surprised when I woke up to sunshine. I found Jake at an ATM in the lobby, stabbing the keypad.

"The password isn't working. I need money." He showed me his empty wallet.

I pulled out his bank card and exchanged it for the credit card he'd stuck in the machine. "Try this one. I'll bet that password you're banging away at will work." I watched the pile of bills slide out. "What are you doing? You don't need to carry around a wad of cash."

"I like to have spending money." According to his story, Jake had been off work for months. Years? Where had the money been coming from? I told him he was buying breakfast.

I was a cheap date. I had toast and coffee.

Jake ordered pancakes. He'd slept and dressed in clean clothes, and even though he was still unshaven, he'd slicked back the long hair. He was a different man this morning, calm. Shock?

"Can you tell me why you and Nadine didn't stay in touch after you were married?" I asked.

He mopped up syrup with a chunk of pancake. "Because you always tell me what to do."

"Jake, the only time I've gotten in your face has been when you're asking for a bailout." I didn't remind him that once he had the cash, he ignored the advice that came with it.

He pointed his fork at me. "You and Mom both tried to stop me from marrying Joanne."

Joanne? Joanne was ancient history. That marriage had lasted two years; it had to be at least twenty years since they washed up on a rock. At least I'd never said "I told you so" when she walked out on him.

"Jake, I can barely remember Joanne. I was there whenever you needed me, and it looks like you need me now."

"I need to go home. Nadine will be wondering where I am."

FIRST, we let a crew with mops and pails into the house. I called the medical supply company, and they said they would be able to take away the sick room furnishings later in the afternoon. Then a haircut and shave for Jake. He looked almost like the handsome old Jake by the time we went to the funeral home. After arrangements for the cremation were in order, the woman who'd gently talked him through the details convinced Jake that an urn would be more fitting for his beloved wife than a cardboard box.

It was too much. I handed him a tissue to wipe away the tears and snot. Nothing on their shelf was pretty enough. He remembered an elephant-shaped cookie jar.

By the time we got back to the house, the key was in the mailbox, and the place smelled of soap and hard work. Someone had lined up an army of prescription bottles on the bathroom counter, all of them Nadine's. I scooped them into a bag and dropped them at a pharmacy when I left Jake and went out to get some basic groceries.

The hospital bed was on its way out when I got back. I'd thought this would be a trigger for tears, but Jake was standing in the kitchen holding an elephant cookie jar, staring at it as though he was in a trance.

"Listen, Jake. I need to go home for some clothes and a few other things." Even more, I desperately needed to get out of this house and away from him, however briefly. "You understand that I'm coming back, right? You don't have to do this alone." I set a bag of groceries in front of him.

He shook his head as though he'd just gained consciousness. "Sure, Pete. That'll be good."

Now what? Shake hands? Fist bumps? We weren't huggers, and never had been. I waved and headed for the door.

I drove home in the dark.

Heather had already begun to plan Jake's future. She was trying to imagine, she said, what Nadine would have wanted for him. I didn't want to imagine anything about Nadine. What I would wonder for a very long time, though, was why she married him and how she turned him into a limp rag.

"Look," I told her, "so far as I've seen, the two of them were isolated by choice. Apparently, that's what Nadine wanted for him."

"That was when they were together. Remember the old gregarious Jake? Do you think she changed him so much that he wants to be a recluse?"

"I think they got married and he moved into Nadine's life. No, she made some space for him."

"Peter, now you're judging the woman and we never knew her, or the pair of them." She paused, bit her lip, and narrowed her eyes the way she does when she's puzzling over something. "Can he live there without her? I should do some research on alternatives."

Research. My wife's organized approach to life. I shrugged. "Sure. That's a great idea."

I didn't tell her I'd done a bit of research myself before I left. I'd knocked on the neighbour's door. She didn't know that Nadine, whom she referred to as "the wife," had been ill. She'd only spoken occasionally with Jake, and he'd mentioned nothing. She smiled. "He once told me, though, that he used to have a dog like mine, and from time to time, he's hung a juicy steak bone on my doorknob." We exchanged phone numbers, and she said she'd keep an eye out for Jake. But she was rarely at home.

Heather wanted to come along when I went back to Jake two days later. I told her this was purely business. We'd see a lawyer, go to the bank, and get a better idea of where we were going, he and I.

Jake answered the door after just one stab at the doorbell. I'd phoned as soon as I got into the city and asked him to be ready to go out, but he still needed to shower. While he was in the bathroom, I prowled around the house. Elephants everywhere, in every room but Jake's office, where the only "art" was a set of photos of the golden retriever he'd had long ago. Throughout the rest of the house, tiny circus elephants, bookends, carvings, paintings, glass figurines. Elephants everywhere. Unlike Heather, who thought this collection was charming and wondered if Jake would give her one of the figurines when I texted her some pictures, I found it just plain creepy.

In the room that was obviously Nadine's office, next to a photo of her in safari clothes, there was a clay model of a mother elephant, much smaller than the one from the living room. Head down, her trunk was curled around the baby leaning against her front legs. I took it off the shelf.

When Jake emerged, I held up the sculpture. "Can Heather have this? You two must have really loved elephants."

"They're from her travelling," Jake said. One of the few forth-right explanations for anything in the house.

"Where did you travel?"

"We didn't. Nadine and her first husband flew all over the world." He glanced at the piece in my hands. "Yeah, take it. I don't need elephants."

"Nadine was married before? You didn't tell us that."

"It was private. She didn't want me to talk about it. He died."

And yet, he was surprisingly forthcoming. Nadine and her first husband had been married for "like" ten years. He was killed in a motorcycle accident. Jake and Nadine met in a pub, "maybe" six months after. She was there with friends, and so was he. "You know how that goes." No, I didn't. Heather and I met in a university chemistry class. "Why are you being so snoopy?" he asked.

"Only for legal purposes," I told him. Beyond that, unlike Heather, I didn't want to know anything more about the woman and her elephant obsession. They were souvenirs. Mystery solved. Except there was the question Heather would raise. Why so soon after the first one died? This isn't uncommon after divorce, but someone who's grieving? After ten years of marriage?

We went to the bank where Nadine's will and Jake's own

were stowed in a safety deposit box. I asked the teller who'd taken us to the boxes if she could find out if Nadine and Jake had a financial adviser. Indeed, they did, and the woman happened to be free. She offered her condolences and showed us into her office. Without the death certificate or will, she couldn't give Jake access to any of the accounts except for one that was in his name —the one he'd been trying to crack in the hotel lobby. *There's always money, and I just take out whatever I need.*

From the point of view of curtailing Jake's spending habits and the cavalier attitude he'd had about money, he'd married the right woman. No debts or encumbrances, and some good investments—no details at this point, but the adviser could offer assurance that Jake was in good shape for the future.

That bank account of Jake's, if he did another withdrawal like the one from the hotel, would hit rock bottom very soon. He thought it would be a good plan if we had two accounts. One that was just his and one that was joint. "That way," he said, "you can look after paying the bills and all that from the joint account, and I can take money out of the other one when I need it." And where would that money come from? I'd keep topping it up just like Nadine did.

Jake had obviously had enough sleep. He seemed tuned into everything we were doing, compliant up to this point, but we had yet to discuss the house.

On to the lawyer. A bit odd, she said, that everything was in Nadine's name; house, car, investments. However, this was fairly straightforward. Jake was the executor as well as sole beneficiary.

"I don't know how to be an executor," he said. "Pete's going to have to do that."

I shrugged, she shrugged back at me, and it appeared we could carry on with dispersing Nadine's estate. The funeral home had seen to registering Nadine's death and would forward the death certificate to the lawyer.

I asked for a glass of water as we were leaving and swallowed two headache tablets. In the car, Jake asked again about money. How much did he have?

"You're in good shape."

"I am? How rich am I?"

"Rich enough."

I dragged him through the grocery store, and we bought enough to feed him until he felt like going out to shop for himself.

Jake was calm and said that he'd be okay on his own, but wouldn't it be better if he came home with me?

"Better if you're here," I told him. Just in case something needed signing in order for him to have money in that account of his. "I'll call every couple of days, or you can phone me if you need something," I told him. "Maybe call someone and get out of the house, even if it's just for coffee. I think Ron and some of the other cousins would like to hear from you."

"Yeah, maybe I'll do that."

It had been a long day. Nine hours with my brother. Although it was dark, on this trip, the roads were clear. I had the elephants on the passenger seat, and every time I glanced that way, an eye was staring at me. When I stopped to get coffee, I put them in the back and covered them with my jacket.

Heather thought the elephant mother and baby were lovely. She placed them on an end table in the living room. Sad as it was, she said, she looked forward to helping Jake find a home for Nadine's treasures, no matter how many there were.

She was shocked that I didn't plan to go back for a month.

"What can I do?" I asked. "I'm not sleeping in that house. Should I stay in the hotel again and take him out to a movie?"

She shook her head. "What about the will, probate, getting his affairs settled?"

"We've signed everything that needed to be signed, and the other documents are in order. I can look after his business from here."

"No memorial service for Nadine? Celebration of her life?"

"Heather, according to Jake, there doesn't seem to be anyone who'd remember her." The funeral home would deliver Nadine's ashes, and it was up to Jake to transfer her to the cookie jar. I'd shaken it and dumped a sleeve of broken Chips Ahoy.

My phone calls lasted no more than five minutes. Heather's "wellness checks," as she called them, were longer. "What did you have for lunch today, Jake? It's four o'clock in the afternoon. How can you not remember? Have you gone out for groceries? Go to the kitchen and open the fridge." A brief pause and then, "Tell me what's on the top shelf. Are those boxes empty? How long have they been there? Throw them out!"

She covered the phone with her hand. "Peter, he's living on takeout food! If he won't leave the house, I'm going to order some groceries for him." She kept him on the phone and walked him down every aisle in the grocery store. There weren't many stops: milk, bread, eggs, cereal, Pepsi, and at the end, he surprised her when he asked for a steak. "I like to barbecue," he said.

"Well, that sounds really fine, Jake, and you'll have everything you need for breakfasts. Call me when the groceries are delivered, and when you want another order, we'll work on that together."

"I don't think so," he said." I don't want you checking up on me. And I don't need Pete to come up here and poke around in our business again." He hung up.

Heather looked as though she'd been slapped.

"Ignore it. It's like he has three or four recorded statements in his head, and no control over what comes out of his mouth." I felt a bit sick, because this was not my jokey younger brother, nor the new, sad and compliant Jake. This was angry Jake, husband of Nadine, who did not want anyone meddling.

"I don't think he's safe living there on his own." She was all but wringing her hands. "Peter, we need to go to Edmonton. Maybe it would be easier if he moved down here." She'd done her research on independent living arrangements in Edmonton.

The one she thought would suit Jake had a sister facility in Calgary.

"Then I can run over every day and look after him? Heather! I'm already my brother's keeper. I don't want to be his nurse-maid!" I swung my arms wide, and the elephant pair on the table next to me was caught in the arc.

She knelt on the hardwood floor, gathering the pieces.

"I am not gluing *that* animal back together either." I knew how nasty I sounded. I also knew Nadine's house would eventually collapse, and we'd move ahead from there.

A WEEK LATER, I phoned Jake's neighbour.

"I haven't seen him out walking, and there doesn't seem to be activity over there," she told me. "I did find a steak in my mailbox a while back." So the groceries had arrived, and he had been outside, if only to take a treat to the dog.

Two more weeks, and then I phoned, and phoned, and phoned. The kind neighbour knocked on Jake's door. No response. The police agreed to do a wellness check. Jake was in the house, they said, but in rough shape. And so, we were back at the beginning.

Before I went back to Edmonton, I needed to be sure there was an option to that damn house. I asked Heather to call the seniors' warehouse she'd visited, get the info on the one in Edmonton, and tell them we'd take whatever was available. Give them a deposit to hold it.

The next day, I found Jake slumped over the kitchen table with his head in his hands. "Why have you been hiding?"

He moaned at me to leave him alone; his head hurt so bad. He was sure he was having a stroke—how it was with Nadine. "I need one of her pain pills, but they're all gone."

I got an appointment with the doctor whose number was on a list tacked beside the phone. He had no idea about Jake's previous health and waved away any serious possibilities so far as the headache was concerned. He'd only agreed to see Jake because I told the receptionist this was an emergency, and he'd been Nadine's doctor. He was brusque to the point of being rude. "You're dehydrated," he told Jake, "and you look like you've been parked for way too long. Keep a full water glass beside you. Get out and get some fresh air." He turned to me. "You might want to have some cognitive testing done."

Then to the lawyer again. Not a sound out of Jake before he scratched his signature on the bottom of the document giving me power of attorney. "Are you sure about this?" she asked.

"What's to think about?" he said when he slid the papers across the desk. "My brother's always in charge." He looked directly at me for a moment. "I guess we like it that way."

I clenched my teeth. Did we?

The woman behind the desk raised her eyebrows.

"My brother wants help with selling his house and dealing with his finances. It's all a bit difficult for him."

Jacob nodded. No reaction to the mention of selling the house?

When we were back in the car, I turned sideways in my seat. "Jake, do you agree that selling the house is a good idea?"

He looked at me as though I'd asked him if the sky was blue. "Nadine said I'm not safe here without her." *Thank you, Nadine! At last!* "She said you and Heather will want me to live with you. She said you'd be happy that I could pay you. I have enough money, right?"

Oh, you sly bitch. "Jake, that's not going to work, but we've checked out some places where you can have your own suite, and there's a dining room for your meals. Even shuffleboard, and cribbage, and lots of folks to talk to. Maybe they even go out to curl. You always loved curling." I was reaching pretty desperately with that one.

He needed a shower. And a haircut. He pushed greasy strands behind his ears. "I'm not going to some old people's graveyard. Like the place you put Mom. I walked by once and saw all those people lined up in wheelchairs out front. No way could I go in and see her like that."

"No, Jake. That was a nursing home. The place I'm talking about is for seniors who can look after themselves—upscale. Heather's even said she'd be happy living there." I wasn't above lying, and that bit of deceit got him nodding, albeit without enthusiasm.

I called a realtor, who arrived with astonishing speed. Even though I'd gathered up takeout containers and scraps on the counters, the stink was still in the room. I suggested the two of us work through the details outside. We went out to her car, and while we were there, I noticed the curtains part next door. I saluted, and the woman waved back.

When the agreement to sell was complete, we went into the house. Jake had turned on the television and was staring at the screen. The sound was muted. I stood in front of him and held out the clipboard and a pen. He finally looked up and took both. The realtor stood quietly by.

He flipped through the pages, squinting. "I'll get good money for the house?"

"Absolutely." The signature finally made it onto the page.

Just like that, we were alone again. I looked around the room. "Okay, I'm taking all this garbage out, but we need to have some cleaners come in so the place shows well."

"I don't want people in here." Jake stood up and folded his arms over his chest. "No way. Nadine and I don't like strangers coming in."

"Jake, this woman can't sell the house unless people can see it. She says it will go fast. It's a pretty little house." Wasn't that the perfect description for Nadine's home? The realtor had also said it would go fast because I'd agreed to a quick-sale price tag. And Jake had signed the agreement.

"Here's what we're going to do. I'll tell the salesperson to hold off on bringing anyone through until you're in the new place. Heather will come up with me, and we'll clean out the house. You can tell me what you want to do with all of this." I waved my arms. "What you want to give away and what you want to keep. The new place has all the furniture you need."

His face contorted. "I don't want any of it. None of this stuff is mine."

He flew into his office and came back with the old photos of his Goldy. "I always thought I'd get another boy like this one," he said. "Nadine doesn't like dogs. Just goddamn elephants." He tucked the faded souvenirs into the pocket of his jeans.

AND HERE WE ARE. We will finish this job if it takes superhuman endurance, and it will. I've booked rooms for two nights at the heartbreak hotel. For today, we've insisted that Jake stay at the hotel while Heather and I clean. Tomorrow, he can come and help us sort out what's left.

Before we leave the hotel, I phone Collingwood Manor to check that everything is in order for Jake's move. It is not. They have a phone call noted, but no deposit and no intake information. They do have a vacancy.

"Why?" I ask Heather. "I thought this was done."

She clears her throat. "I put a deposit on the one at home. Let's see how things stand at the end of tomorrow, Peter."

She's been watching from the sidelines, with no sense of what's been going on, other than her commitment to do what's right for little brother Jake. "I hope it's refundable because we're going right now to put that deposit on Jake's new Edmonton digs."

That mission accomplished, we go to the house, two hours behind already. I try to convince Heather to go for a walk while I sweep the kitchen debris into garbage bags, spray the surfaces with disinfectant, and open the windows. She will not. And neither has her face softened since she walked through the house and saw the pitiful pile of belongings Jake was taking with him. "He's more absent from this house than she is." Her voice is flat. "Let's just get this done."

We don masks and vinyl gloves, and without even checking to see if there are plates or cutlery in the mess, we pull handfuls of trash off the kitchen counter and fill garbage bags.

Today we clean and sort, tomorrow I have trucks coming, one from a charitable organization that will take away the furniture, and another for the junk. Jake thinks we're selling it all.

What do we do if Nadine gets into his head and he blows up when we start loading her treasures? Rent a storage unit, an extra-large urn for these remains? Nadine is in the cookie jar. It's ugly: big enough to hold a loaf of bread, and the elephant has a creepy smile. I have no idea where Jake stowed it.

First, we pack up the kitchen: dishes, pots and pans, all manner of utensils, and small appliances are in boxes stacked against the wall. About two hours into the job, I notice that Heather is carrying each of the elephant shrines to the island in the kitchen. When her arm catches a small herd on the edge of the counter, she gets a broom and sweeps the pieces into a dust pan.

A similar mishap befalls one that I find truly ugly when I reach to lift it off a shelf in the kitchen. I realize that I haven't seen the family of four since I moved them out of the living room the first time I was in the house. "Do you want any of these?" I ask.

"I don't want anything that belongs to the woman in this house."

After the kitchen, we clear the bathroom. Then we empty every dresser, desk, and bookcase onto the floors and line up furniture in the hallway. It's been seven hours since we began, with just a short break to eat the fruit and cheese and crackers Heather packed. She is shaking.

"Coffee." I go out and I'm back in ten minutes with two large cups with extra cream and sugar. We sit on the front step letting the caffeine do what it can, and then walk up the block and back just to remind us the world is out there—not inside Nadine's house.

It's time to quit for today. There are boxes and boxes; the ones at the back step will go on the junk truck; the ones stacked in the living room will go to the thrift store. Neither of us has pondered the fate of any item for more than a few seconds. We'll deal with everything in the closets and on the floor in Nadine's office in the morning.

When Heather goes out to the car, I take a large box into the kitchen for the elephants. With luck, the ones we *saved* will be gone from this well-travelled alley by morning. "Heather," I ask when I get into the car, "did you see that big family of elephants? I sent you a picture, remember?"

She shakes her head.

Jake is in the hotel coffee shop. "Is it done?" he asks.

Heather has run out of the sad affection she showered on Jake when we arrived. She shakes her head in disbelief. "Done?"

"Tomorrow," I tell him. "We'll finish tomorrow." Then I ask, "Jake, where are those big elephants that used to be in the living room?"

"I dunno," he says. "I guess Nadine gave them to somebody."

Heather orders a sandwich to take upstairs, and I sit down and eat with Jake. When I go up to our room, she's asleep. She's flung the jeans and shirt she was wearing onto the floor and is curled on her side in the bed in her underwear. The sandwich, unopened, is in the bathroom, where the only other evidence of her being there is her wet toothbrush. Both of us are seventy years old. I have no idea how we summoned the energy to do this furious demolition.

I wake up to Heather storming around the room. She's eaten the sandwich from last night and says all she needs is coffee to go. If Jake and I want food, we'd better get it now. She's leaving in twenty minutes, and she is *not* staying another night. She's still in overdrive.

When we get to the house, the truck for the furniture is already there. The "1-800-Got Junk?" and thrift store trucks will come in the afternoon. I check the back lane to see if someone has carried away the box of delightful elephants, and it has disappeared, but when I turn to go back inside, I see it on a garden bench near the door. I was too tired to walk the intended distance to the gate last night?

For Heather, clearing Nadine's closet doesn't require any decisions other than thrift store. I'm dumbstruck when Jake urges Heather to try on a pair of shoes, boots, some of the clothes. Why this burst of generosity after the protectionism?

Simple answer. He's sure Nadine would rather the "gifts" go to Heather than to strangers. I almost see the lavish generosity of old Jake.

Heather puts a hand on his shoulder. "No thanks, Jake. There's nothing here that's to my taste." She swoops it all, still on hangers, and carries it into the living room.

I was afraid Nadine's office would be Pandora's Box, but it's relatively straightforward. We pack jewellery, scarves, pieces of luggage. Jake leaves the room while we fill another giveaway box.

Finally, the only items left are in the back of the closet, a cardboard gift box and a metal one with a combination lock. I call Jake. "Do you know what's in the safe?"

He shakes his head. "Personal stuff, I guess."

"Would there be legal papers, anything like that?"

Again, he shakes his head.

"I'll take it home just to be sure."

"No. I don't want you to take her private stuff home." Back and forth we go, from one Jake to another Jake. He goes out to the kitchen and comes back with a hammer. His arm is strong. One good smash on the lock and it cracks.

Personal documents: ex-husband's birth certificate, driver's licence, passport, death certificate, marriage licence for the two of them. In the other box, there are travel brochures and photos, so many happy photos of the two of them around the world. He was a handsome man, this Philip whose existence we've just exhumed.

I grab Jake's arm when he reaches for a black garbage bag. "Not the documents. I'll take them home and shred them." He scoops up the travel memories and ties the bag off with a double knot. Landfill.

Heather points to the top shelf. "There's something else up there in the corner." I only have to give the white cardboard box a shake to know what it is. It's sealed with tape, just like the one that was delivered to Jake from the funeral home.

"He can stay here. It was his house." Stunned, the two of us watch from the back door as Jake goes out and dumps the remains of Philip Harrington in a bed of shrubs along the garage wall.

Both trucks have arrived. The driver from the thrift store truck assures us that his load will go to grateful people. He's excited about that collection of elephants Heather has carried in from the backyard. He says he just might take those home to his wife.

The two from the other truck give each other quick glances as they load items that I know should have a destination other than the landfill, but I haven't the strength to think about it, nor to feel guilty. "You sure about all this?" one of them asks. "You could get good money for some of this stuff."

"Absolutely sure. Take out whatever you want," I tell them, "and come back after work and pick it up." I close and lock the back door.

Inside, Heather leans into me, and I put my arms around her. "A job well done, Peter," she says. "But will you regret it later?"

"Disposing of Nadine's home? Not a chance. Leaving Jake up here and hoping for the best? Who knows?"

"I'll get a refund," she whispers.

My brother is sitting on the front step, leaning back on his hands. He has a suitcase and the large cookie jar on the step below him.

Heather taps on the jaunty hat that is the lid on the elephant. "What's this?" she asks him.

"Nadine," he says.

She shakes her head. I don't tell her that it's not just a souvenir.

When Jake stands, he points to the weeping willow. "There they are," he says.

"What's there?" I ask.

"The mama elephant and her babies."

Heather takes my arm and pulls me away. "Nothing but weeds," she whispers. I'm not tempted to look back.

Each of us offers him a hand.

"Come on, Jacob," I say. "Let's get you home."

ACKNOWLEDGMENTS

Some of the stories in this collection were written over a span of almost twenty years. Others are new, or as new as a story can be after a fifth or sixth draft, when it's time to let go and type "END."

I am indebted to Shirley Black for her generosity, encouragement, and wisdom since my earliest years of writing. To the many other readers on whom I've inflicted various drafts, warm thanks for your sharp eyes and insight. Peter Midgley's endorsement and editing of these stories gave me the push I needed when I needed it most. Particular thanks are due, as always, to Dave Margoshes for years of friendship and mentorship of the highest order.

These are works of fiction. My family—Robert, Elisabeth and Barb, Eric, and Stefan—will recognize, as they always do, the influence they've had and the moments I've stolen from their lives. They enrich my life and my writing.

I thank Edward Willett and Shadowpaw Press for putting these stories between covers.

My thanks to the editors who have published some of these stories previously:

- "The Queen is Coming." Broadcast on CBC Radio's *Alberta Anthology* and published in *The Best of Alberta Anthology* (2005).
- "Unmasked." Published online by *Agnes and True* (2022).

- "Dressed for the Occasion." An earlier version was published in *Room* (2008).
- "Kick." Published in *Dark Times,* edited by Ann Walsh (Ronsdale Press, 2005).
- "Jewel." Published in *Freefall* (2018).
- "Party Favours." Published in CPL story vending machine, and published in *Tap Press Read 1-3-5* (Loft on Eighth, 2020).
- "A Practical Woman" and "Trespasses" in *A Crack in the Wall* (Oolican Books 2008)

ABOUT BETTY JANE HEGERAT

Calgary author Betty Jane Hegerat was a social worker in a long-ago life. The stories she has written since leaving that career behind reflect an ongoing need to make sense of conflict and chaos in relationships and to find moments of laughter and even glimmers of redemption.

That seriousness aside, she loves the Calgary writing community. She has taught at the Alexandra Writers' Centre and the Fernie Writers' Conference, and at Continuing Education at the University of Calgary, and was Writer in Residence for the Calgary Public Library. In 2015, she was honoured to receive the Writers Guild of Alberta Golden Pen Award for lifetime achievement in writing. Betty Jane's stories have been published in anthologies, magazines.

She has five previous books: a novel, *Running Toward Home* (Newest Press), a collection of stories, *A Crack in the Wall* (Oolichan Books), a novel, *Delivery* (Oolican Books), a YA novel, *Odd One Out* (Oolichan Books) and *The Boy* (Oolichan Books). *The Boy* is a French braid of investigative journalism, fiction, memoir, and meta-fiction. The book was shortlisted for the Calgary Book Prize, High Plains Book Awards, and Alberta Writers Guild Wilfrid Eggleston Non-Fiction award.

ABOUT SHADOWPAW PRESS

Shadowpaw Press is a traditional publishing company, located in Regina, Saskatchewan, Canada and founded in 2018 by Edward Willett, an award-winning author of science fiction, fantasy, and non-fiction for readers of all ages. A member of Literary Press Group (Canada) and the Association of Canadian Publishers, Shadowpaw Press publishes an eclectic selection of books by both new and established authors, including adult fiction, young adult fiction, children's books, non-fiction, and anthologies, plus new editions of notable, previously published books in any genre.

Email: publisher@shadowpawpress.com.

facebook.com/shadowpawpress
x.com/shadowpawpress
instagram.com/shadowpawpress

ALSO FROM SHADOWPAW PRESS

Literary Fiction

Hello by David Carpenter

Theories of Everything by Dwayne Brenna

The Laundryman by Dwayne Brenna

The Lavender Child by Harriet Richards

Waiting for the Piano Tuner to die by Harriet Richards

Let us be True by Erna Buffie

Dollybird by Anne Lazurko

Small Reckonings by Karin Melberg Schwier

Thickwood by Gayle M. Smith

Poetry

First Light, Last Light by Glen Sorestad

The Door at the End of Everything by Lynda Monahan

The Glass Lodge: 20th Anniversary Edition by John Brady McDonald

Phases by Belinda Betker

Stay by Katherine Lawrence

Nonfiction

The Crow Who Tampered With Time by Lloyd Ratzlaff

Backwater Mystic Blues by Lloyd Ratzlaff

Cupboard Love: A Dictionary of Culinary Curiosities by Mark Morton

9 781998 273485